DOUBLE JEOPARDY

A NOVEL OF ROMANTIC SUSPENSE

JUDITH BLEVINS

Cover, interior book design, and eBook design
by Blue Harvest Creative
www.blueharvestcreative.com

DOUBLE JEOPARDY

Published by
Shahrazad Publishing

ISBN-13: 978-0692677117
ISBN-10: 0692677119

Visit the author at:
www.bhcauthors.com

Visit the author by
scanning the QR code.

OTHER TITLES BY JUDITH BLEVINS

Karma

The Legacy

Swan Song

DEDICATION

This novel is dedicated to those who have accompanied me on my life's journey and, despite the many challenges, never left my side.

ACKNOWLEDGMENTS

To all those who encouraged and inspired me to write this novel I am most grateful. Special thanks to my daughter, Shelly Blevins-Lambert, my treasured friend, Pamela Cotharn, and to my favorite mystery and legal fiction writer, Carroll Multz. Carroll's sage advice and editing skills contributed greatly to making this novel what it is.

TABLE OF CONTENTS

Prologue...15

PART ONE ...and so it begins...

Chapter 1 – Clear and Sunny........................21

Chapter 2 – Slightly Breezy..........................37

Chapter 3 – Whirlwinds................................47

Chapter 4 – Cloudy Skies.............................56

Chapter 5 – Cold Front.................................66

PART TWO ...and so it continues...

Chapter 6 – Gathering Clouds.....................85

PART THREE ...and so it ends...

Chapter 7 – Severe Storms..........................101

Chapter 8 – Turbulence...............................118

Chapter 9 – Wind and Rain.........................128

Chapter 10 – Scattered Showers...................137

Chapter 11 – Unseasonably Warm...........147

Chapter 12 – Below Freezing.....................157

Chapter 13 – Flash Flooding.....................178

Chapter 14 – Clear Skies.............................185

Chapter 15 – Hurricane Warnings............197

Epilogue..225

DOUBLE
JEOPARDY

I am the master of my fate; I am the captain of my soul.
~ *Invictus* – William Henley ~

PROLOGUE

T he big show was about to begin and Jordan Slater and her boyfriend, Dave Jennings, scrunched up against the wall adjacent to the floor-to-ceiling glass window where they could watch the crew from the national weekly television program, *Sincerely Yours*, juggle their gear into place. The sound team swarmed about wiring the participants with mics and the cameramen jockeyed for position setting up their shot angles.

Linda Bishop, star reporter for *Sincerely Yours*, had placed Samuel "Salty" Morton behind his modest oak desk and, as makeup was being applied, she continuously barked orders at her staff while simultaneously giving Salty instructions on how the interview would be conducted.

Samuel "Salty" Morton derived the nickname "Salty" initially from the time he spent as a JAG officer with the Navy. Since sailors are known as salts and with a last name of Morton, the moniker just seemed to fit. When he left the Navy and went into private practice, the nickname stuck. It didn't take long for Salty to develop a reputation in the private sector and he was soon equated with the elements of salt. He was known in the legal arena for his ability to not make much ado about nothing and to *take things with a grain of salt*. His level-headed-ness made *salt of the earth* an appropriate description. He certainly *earned his salt* as his dedication to his clients was legendary and, of course, he was theatrical enough to *add flavor* to any court hearing.

Not to be outdone, Mother Nature had lent a hand as well when she determined he should become prematurely gray. Thus when he was 26 years of age his hair started gradually turning and now in his sixties was completely white. The thick unruly mass perched atop his head gave way to vivid blue eyes that never disclosed what he was thinking but could delve deep into another's and determine what was hidden beyond. He was teased that he could have made a fortune playing poker.

Morton, although mature, was still handsome in that "Clark Gable" way, mustache and all. He sported broad shoulders and his athletic build was enhanced by his inviting smile and hypnotic voice. He was Navy tough and military rigid. His demeanor transmitted the message he was not to be toyed with and not many challenged him physically. Those who did regretted it. Salty's integrity was irreproachable and he was highly respected by members of the local bar including prosecutors, defense attorneys and judicial personnel.

BISHOP REACHED DOWN and extracted a hand mirror from her purse which was positioned snugly at her feet. Sitting beside Salty discussing the interview questions, she tilted her head from side-to-side examining her makeup. She then fumbled a tube of lipstick from her makeup pouch and applied a fresh coat to her lips.

Suddenly bright lights flooded the office. Salty jerked his head up and blinked. He was almost blinded by the lights and rubbed his eyes. Before he could clear the barrage of spots dancing before his vision, Bishop gave the thumbs-up to her crew to proceed. The cameramen honed in on her and the filming began.

In her practiced "on air" voice as she gazed into the camera, Bishop launched into the introduction of the *Sincerely Yours* interview.

She began, "I'm here in Farmington, New Mexico with this year's winner of the prestigious defense bar's *Lifetime Achievement Award.*" She then put her hand on Salty's arm which was resting on the desk, and continued, "A panel, consisting of a variety of legal experts including judges, prosecutors, defense attorneys, legislators and public officials, review the nominees' qualifications. To even be considered for this award is an honor in itself." Bishop turned and smiled at Salty. Salty, still fighting with the spots, smiled back. "The members of the *Lifetime Achievement* panel selected Trial Attorney Samuel Morton to receive this year's honor. His brilliant career, spanning more than four decades, is highlighted by the defense of the innocent who may have otherwise been convicted of crimes they had not committed."

Bishop casually flipped her long blond hair back from her face. After a slight pause, she continued, "Mr. Morton, better known among his collogues as "Salty," is here for an exclusive interview with *Sincerely Yours.*" She turned toward Salty and asked, "Sir, may I call you Salty?"

Salty, trying not to look self-conscious, leaned back in his chair before answering, "Of course. I'm rarely referred to by any other name and may not recognize to whom you are speaking if you continue to call me Mr. Morton and, please, Ms. Bishop, drop the 'Sir,' I left that behind when I left the Navy."

"Okay, Salty it is but then you must call me Linda," Bishop laughed and glanced down at her notes. Looking up again, she said, "Over the span of your forty-plus-year career you have undoubtedly dealt with many clients and situations too numerous to list. With this in mind, we previously asked you to select one special case, a case that stands out in your memory that you would like to focus on in this interview. Although I'm certain you have had many exciting cases, time constraints limit us to focusing on just one." Bishop looked up and smiled into the camera. "I'm now going to turn this interview over to Salty and let him tell us, in his own words, about the most fascinating case of his career."

"Thank you, Linda," Salty said and looked into the camera. His gaze went beyond the camera lens and he appeared to be looking into the past. The cameraman pulled back slightly giving a wider angle of the office and captured Bishop as she sat transfixed with her chin resting on her thumb and forefinger waiting for Salty to begin. The motion of the cameraman brought Salty back to the present.

IN PREPARING FOR the interview, Salty had relived the events that led up to the most notorious trial, not only of his career, but also of San Juan County's. He had selected the first degree murder case of *People of the State of New Mexico v. Jasmine Zachary*. Having near-photographic memory, even tiny details loomed large in his mind. Intertwining his fingers on the desk before him, Salty cleared his throat preparing to speak. He pressed his lips together for a moment and exhaled slowly as the memories, still vivid, took shape in his mind.

PART ONE
...AND SO IT BEGINS...

1
CLEAR AND SUNNY

It was the end of July and New Mexico was living up to the predicted promise of being hot–miserably hot in fact. In Farmington, Holy Trinity's five o'clock Saturday evening mass was no exception. Jas noticed the church was not as crowded as usual. She reasoned that many church-goers were probably vacationing or planning to attend the much cooler Sunday morning masses.

A creature of habit, Jas always closed her interior design shop early in order to get to mass by five. Living alone and having been widowed several years before, she seldom deviated from her routine. It was a relief to get her religious obligation out of the way so she could lounge around on Sunday, her only day off.

The July heat pressed in upon the congregation and the mass droned on and on with the redundant sermon. Hot and bored, Jas took a tissue from her pocket and blotted the perspiration from her upper lip. As she stuffed the wadded tissue back into her pocket, she glanced around at her fellow worshipers. Jas froze when she looked across the aisle. Her eyes fixed on a familiar face from the past and her mind filled with memories. *Could that possibly be Nick McGregor?* She stared at the man as he knelt, head bowed in prayer. Jas began conjuring up images from forty years before when she was a freshman at Farmington High School. She remembered having a serious school-girl crush on Nick McGregor at that time.

Jas' reverie was interrupted and she was jerked back into the present when the priest began chanting, "Glory be to the Father, the Son and the Holy Spirit..." She, however, still had the man in her sight when he suddenly raised his head and looked at her. Exhibiting discomfort, he hiked up his collar and gestured toward himself as if to say "are you staring at me?" Jas immediately looked away and buried her head in her folded hands hoping to hide her red-faced embarrassment. *Good grief, what must he be thinking even if that were Nick, I wonder if he even recognized me?* When mass finally ended, Jas grabbed her bag, slung it over her shoulder and hurried from the church hoping not to humiliate herself any further.

THE LONG, HOT summer wore on and July was almost history. The man with the familiar face continued to be present at five o'clock mass always sitting in his now familiar pew. Not wanting to attract attention to herself, Jas tried to ignore him by keeping her eyes down pretending to read from her prayer book. However, she couldn't keep from stealing glances every so often. *After all, forty years can change one's appearance and that may not even be Nick.*

On the last Saturday in July, as Jas exited the church, she saw the person she believed to be Nick McGregor leaning against the hand rail as he stood on the church steps chatting with other parishioners. She tucked her head attempting to hurry past but was stopped midstride when a pleasant male voice called out, "Say, aren't you Jasmine O'Connor?"

She turned around to see a friendly smile gracing her mysterious stranger's handsome face as he descended the steps and approached her.

"You look so familiar," he said. "Did you go to Farmington High?"

A twinge of excitement rippled through the pit of her stomach as she returned his smile and extended her hand. It *was* Nick McGregor.

"Why yes. I thought I recognized you as well. It's been a long time but you don't seem to have changed much."

He chuckled pleasantly at the compliment. "I'm flattered that you think so, but my mirror tells me otherwise."

"Well then," Jas assured him, "you need a new mirror."

Nick threw up his hands in mock surrender, "I don't like to tempt fate." His eyes twinkled as he said, "Remember what happened to Snow White when the wicked stepmother's mirror turned on her?"

Jas' heart was fluttering like a hummingbird's wings. She jokingly replied, "Okay then, your lesson for today is to just avoid apples."

"Good advice!" Nick hesitated a moment as he held her in his gaze. "It suddenly occurs to me that my education in fairytales is somewhat lacking. Perhaps I could persuade you to join me for dinner so you can enlighten me on how to dodge poison apples and other pitfalls." He flashed his captivating smile once again. "Besides, I'd love to get to know you better and catch up with what's been going on in your life."

That was the quintessential heart-stopping moment. Jas answered hoping her voice wasn't quivering, "I'd love to have dinner with you, Nick."

"Excellent. Why don't we take my car and I'll bring you back to pick up yours after dinner." Then he hesitated, "That is if that's acceptable to you?"

"Yes, of course. That sounds like a good plan." Jas surprised herself. She was walking and talking but her mind didn't seem to be functioning. Just as if forty years hadn't passed, she was still mesmerized by this man.

Nick escorted her to a polished late model white diamond Cadillac Escalade sitting off by itself in the church parking lot. He opened the passenger door and she slid onto the soft, comfortable leather seat and then watched as he circled the car and climbed in behind the wheel.

Fastening his seatbelt, he asked, "How does the River Side sound to you? The brochures say it's known for its charming elegance and fine food." Nick cautiously looked both directions before exiting the parking lot. "I haven't been there in a while so I can't say one way or the other."

"The brochures are accurate. It's one of my favorite places."

"Then the River Side it is!" Nick smiled and looked in Jas' direction. Jas smiled back wishing her heart would slow down to a normal pace.

THE INTERIOR OF the restaurant was cool and comfortable. After they ordered, their conversation became lively and surprisingly comfortable. They took turns bringing each other up to speed on the last forty years. However, to Jas it was as if they had never been apart.

"Nick, you graduated a year ahead of me," Jas said, "did you go on to college?"

Nick, twisting his wine glass between his thumb and forefinger, replied, "No, I'd had enough school but, as they say, if I had it to do over…"

"Boy, do I know that feeling. What did you do?"

"Well, I'm afraid it's not the stuff stories are made of but after graduation, I did a stint in the Air Force and learned to fly."

"That sounds pretty exciting to me…"

"It was. There's no thrill to compare to flying. I discovered flying was in my blood, and oddly enough, I became addicted to it. When I left the Air Force, I went to work for World Wide Airlines as a captain and flew internationally for the next twenty-five years."

"Now that really sounds exciting. I've barely been out of Farmington all these years."

"Well, my dear, there's a lot to be said about home-life. Maybe it's not exciting but it's comfortable and reliable. The older I get, the more I appreciate stability."

"Where are you living now? I mean with your international contacts, Farmington doesn't seem a likely place to be hanging your hat," Jas asked as she surreptitiously crossed her fingers hoping he did live close.

"Farmington is one of my favorite places. I love it here," Nick replied. "Stephanie and I made our home here. I commuted to Albuquerque a couple of times a month when I flew. I'm now retired, and as the saying goes, living the dream."

Jas blinked in disbelief. *He does live here but, he's married.* Jas' heart sank and she hoped it didn't show so she rushed on. "Do you have children?"

"Yes. I have four daughters and am blessed with seven grandchildren. My daughter, Nicole and her husband, Jeremy, live locally with three of my grandchildren. Molly's twelve, Tony ten and Suzy is eight. My swimming pool may be one reason I get to see them regularly in the summer, otherwise its catch-as-catch can.

"My other daughters are married and scattered across the country. We do try to get together and have a yearly family reunion but there is usually one or two who can't make it. I remember how difficult it was to go places when the kids were in school. Even the summers were filled with running here-and-there participating in sports and other summer activities. My wife, Stephanie, died three years ago from ovarian cancer."

Jas was instantly ashamed of herself because of the elation she felt at finding out Nick's wife had died. She noticed that Nick became quiet and reflective.

Nick was lost in his thoughts. *I can't tell her that after Stephanie died, I became depressed and secluded myself even to the extent of not going to church. I didn't want to be around people. I was har-*

boring guilty feelings. The death of Steph didn't cause my depression; my guilt at having not loved her did. When I came to grips with the guilt I began going back to church and prayed that God and Stephanie would both forgive me for my lack of love for her and the charade our marriage turned into.

Jas shifted in her chair. She watched Nick and waited for him to continue. Nick, suddenly realizing he was distracted said, "You know, since I've retired, I take time to do the things I like to do. Sometimes I rent a puddle-jumper and go see the kids. I should take you up into the wild blue yonder someday and give you the bird's eye view of how enchanting the desert is from the air."

"It sounds wonderful!" exclaimed Jas. "I'd *love* it."

Nick took a sip of his wine and smiled. "Yep, you sure would. Then you'll understand why New Mexico is called *The Land of Enchantment.* Flying over the Grand Canyon is truly a treat. You have no idea of the vastness until you've seen the Colorado River from the air. God must have been in seventh heaven, literally, when He created the Grand Canyon."

Jas, having settled down, became more relaxed. "I've seen pictures in magazines but I'm sure they don't compare to the real thing."

Nick guffawed, "Amen to that. Nothing compares to flying!" Nick took another sip of wine, and gazing into Jas' blue eyes, said, "Say, if you're not in a hurry, after we finish here maybe you would like to drop by my house and see the giant catfish I've been cultivating in a pond on the 'south forty.'"

Another heart-stopping moment. "I would like to. Don't know that I've ever seen *giant catfish.* Are they scary?"

Nick reared back in his chair and laughed. He then leaned forward and whispered, "Yep, Straight out of *Stranger than Fiction* magazine. I believe the article was entitled *The Catfish that Ate Farmington.*"

Jas covered her laugh with her napkin. "Now I'm really fascinated. No reneging, you promised." Then after a pause she added, "You will protect me, won't you?"

"Of course! What kind of host would feed his guest to his *pets*?"

AFTER A PLEASANT dinner, they climbed back into Nick's car, and with the open sunroof exposing the beautiful desert evening sky, drove to the Desert Rose estates where he lived. The massive Spanish-style structure the McGregor's called home was perched on top of the hill and considered a local landmark. The property was surrounded by intricate wrought iron fencing. Jas remembered admiring it from her high school days. Nick nosed the car up the hill along a road that cut through the center of the property.

All along the driveway and fringing the front of the house, perennials were strategically placed and dominated with an explosion of color. Gently swaying Pampas grass and a variety of cacti added drama to the meticulously landscaped grounds. The road opened into a sweeping cobbled drive that widened into a plaza in front of the house. In the center of the plaza was a huge stone fountain with water cascading into a pool at its base which was surrounded by colorful plants.

Nick stopped in front of the house and killed the engine. When he opened the door for Jas, she stepped out and stopped for a moment, pivoting her head back and forth as she tried to take it all in. Xanadu was the first descriptive adjective that popped into Jas's mind. She had often wondered what it would be like to live here and never *dreamed* that she would ever have the chance to go inside.

"Nick, this is more beautiful than I ever imagined!"

Nick smiled as he took her arm and led her onto a massive veranda that ran the full width of the house. They entered through large mahogany hand-carved doors and Jas was greet-

ed by an immense foyer. The polished marble tile floor underscored a high vaulted ceiling painted with colorful mosaics. Jas
embraced the coolness of the entryway as Nick led her through
a wide archway flanked by thick columns and into a comfortable open living room. The entire back wall was set with glass
panels revealing a wide expanse of lawn and a shaded patio
punctuated by a spectacular pool.

"If you'd like the twenty-five-cent tour you can put your
things over there." Nick stabbed his finger toward a large
couch that hugged the curve of the wall.

"I'd love it!" she exclaimed.

"Well okay then. And since you're so enthusiastic, I'll
wave the fee and give you an exclusive, once-in-a-lifetime free
tour," Nick teased as he took her hand.

NICK'S TOUCH SENT Jas' heart racing again and, as if hyp-
notized, she accompanied him from room-to-room. The six bedroom home was tastefully decorated in a Spanish-style theme
to match the architecture. Even though some of the décor was
dated, each room they visited was even lovelier than the last.
The kitchen area seemed to Jas to be larger than her entire condominium. It sported a wide window which spanned the entire
length of the room overlooking an enchanting view of the desert.
The tour continued with a stop in the media room and then into
a comfortable library with a large fireplace, massive overstuffed
furniture and some impressive bronze sculptures. When they
finally settled onto a large canopied swing on the patio adjacent
to the pool, Jas exclaimed, "This is fantastic!" Then looking past
the pool at the expanse of manicured lawn beyond, she said,
"It's like having a city park all to yourself. If I lived here I would
think I had died and gone to heaven."

"It is all that," Nick responded and frowned. "However,
it does have its drawbacks. I just recently lost my live-in maid
due to college graduation. She decided to find a real job and

apply her degree. I'm having trouble finding a replacement. Those who have applied are either too old or too young or don't possess the desired qualifications."

Now Jas frowned. *I wonder if he realizes that his comments are inappropriate or if it's his nature to want to be perceived as the quintessential forty-year-old bachelor.* She tried not to let her disappointment show and replied, "I think I know what you're referring to. Unless they're a ten, you don't want them."

"What? Are you clairvoyant on top of everything else? Looks as though I better be careful not only in what I say but what I think." They both laughed.

After a long thoughtful moment, Jas said, "Our faith teaches us that you can sin in what you think as well as in what you do. Those thoughts about the coveted maid didn't escape me or the Lord."

Looking heavenward, Nick said, "*Mea culpa, mea culpa, mea maxima culpa.*"

Playing along, Jas just shook her head in contrived disgust and said, "You better say a perfect Act of Contrition to be forgiven for your sinfulness."

"I don't think salvation is in the cards. My paradise, as you earlier described it, is here and now." An awkward moment passed and Jas realized it was time to change the subject.

"When did you return to Farmington?" she asked brightly, altering the course of the conversation.

Nick furrowed his brow apparently trying to remember, "We came back shortly after the deaths of my parents. That would be twenty-two years ago this coming January. You no doubt read about my parents being killed in a traffic accident on their way home from a New Year's Eve celebration at the country club."

Jas gently placed her hand over Nick's, and looking into his eyes, said, "I did read about that. What a terrible thing. I think the newspaper said they were the victims of a hit-and-run accident and it was never determined who was responsible."

Nick nodded. Sadness crept into his eyes. "Yes, that's correct. Some days later they interviewed a local drunk who they suspected was involved. However, he cleverly claimed his damaged pickup was stolen. Since it was recovered on the outskirts of town and the drunk's brother vouched for his whereabouts, no arrest was ever made."

Jas, still covering Nick's hand with hers asked, "And so nothing more was done?"

"Right!" Jas detected anger in Nick's voice and didn't want to pursue the matter further. She stood, and putting her hands on her hips, she looked around and remarked, "Nick, this is so lovely. Do you miss Albuquerque?"

"Not really." Nick then rose and stood beside her. They both took in the panorama that was now bathed in twilight as the sun silently slid over the horizon. Nick moved closer to Jas and continued, "I really have always loved Farmington and the home place. Being an only child, I inherited the estate. This is where my heart has always been — guess you could call it my security blanket. The transition was difficult for a time because, after moving back, for years I commuted to Albuquerque, my home base."

"Oh my! That would be a challenge," Jas exclaimed as she turned to look at Nick.

Nick laughed and motioned her back to the swing. "It wasn't a daily trip. Seniority has its privileges and since I flew internationally, I only worked ten days a month which equated to only two round trips per month from Farmington to Albuquerque."

Jas flushed. She was embarrassed at having been so naive. Nick noticed Jas' embarrassment and now it was Nick's turn to redirect the conversation. "Say, I have a fresh pitcher of iced tea. How 'bout a glass?"

Jas smiled. "That sounds good. No sugar, please."

Nick was gone less than five minutes. Returning he sat back down beside her, and as he handed her a glass, he clinked his glass against hers and said, "Here's looking at you, kid."

Jas laughed and, after taking a sip, she said, "One of my favorite lines from one of my favorite movies of all time."

"Mine, too. Well, that is right behind 'Play it once more, Sam.'"

"Close enough," Jas smiled.

Nick smiled back. "So tell me, what have you been up to? Quite obviously, the passage of time hasn't taken its toll on you. You still look fabulous."

Jas blushed and took another sip of tea before saying, "When I read about your parents, I tried to get in touch with you to express my sympathy. Unfortunately, I was unable to obtain your address." Jas paused before adding, "You probably hadn't heard that both of my parents drowned in a boating accident at Lake Powell. So you see, I know how devastating it is to lose both parents at the same time."

"Oh, my God. No, I didn't know and I'm so sorry. When did that happen?"

Jas sat silent for a few moments before replying, "It was ten years ago this Fourth of July."

Nick gently squeezed Jas' arm in a gesture of sympathy. "I never really kept in touch with anyone after high school. This is the first I've learned of your parents' tragic deaths. I'm so sorry."

BOTH SAT IN silent reflection. Finally Nick said, "You haven't told me much about what you've been doing these past years. I remember you from high school. You cut quite the cute figure in your cheerleading outfit. Purple and white, fight, fight, fight!" He threw back his head and laughed. "You know, if I hadn't been going steady with Sandra Dee wanna be," he teased, "I certainly would have dated you even though you were just a freshman puke."

"Ha!" Jas laughed rolling her eyes. "I'm not so sure. In fact, I'd lay odds that you wouldn't have. After all, you were the big man on campus and very popular." Then she sneered, mimicking Nick, "And I was just a freshman puke."

"Now, now, don't be bitter." Then after a slight pause he added, "I figured I'd pay for that last remark," Nick's eyes twinkled in the twilight.

"Haven't you heard the expression 'paybacks are hell?'"

"Ho-ho! Not only have I heard it, I've experienced it… many, many times."

I'll just bet you have. Jas was conflicted. *As much as I want to be with Nick, I dislike his attitude toward women. I suspect he just uses them and then when they were no longer useful or became burdensome, he discards them like yesterday's newspaper. What to do? My head is screaming for me to run but my heart keeps coaxing me to take a chance. Heart wins every time!*

Jas was snapped back to the present when Nick, with a sly smile, continued, "Sandra, of course, thought she was the cat's meow! I suspect having wealth in the family increases one's opinion of one's self." Jas then noticed a change in Nick's voice when he said, "You should've seen her when you were voted Homecoming Queen. She was livid."

"Really!" Jas smiled as she conjured up an image of her moment of glory and of Sandra being livid. *Served her right.*

Gently pushing the swing back and forth, Nick continued the stroll down memory lane.

"One of the fondest memories of my high school years was the time you and I were alone in the school library and you boldly walked up to me and kissed me sweetly on the lips. I still think about that and how that affected me emotionally. It was so unexpected. You were always the shy type. You really threw me for a loop." Nick then grinned as he said, "I almost went into shock. Guess you thought big, bad football heroes were immune to shock?" He raised his eyebrows and smiled. "So, bring me up to speed. What's happened in your life since high school? I've been doing all the talking."

Jas hung on the words *One of the fondest memories...* She was encouraged that perhaps they did have a future. "Well, I admit you were rather dashing in your football uniform and I had a super schoolgirl crush on you. But, I suspect you knew that and, if you didn't, you were deaf, dumb and blind."

Nick continued to gently push the swing. "Yep, that's me!" Then he nudged her leg with his knee, "Go on, this is getting interesting."

Jas playfully punched him on the arm. "As for the kiss, I've been known to be impulsive and spontaneous and that was one of those rare moments. Now that I think about it, you certainly responded to the kiss. You recovered rather quickly from the 'shock.'" Jas pursed her lips and rubbed her chin lightly. "And, you still think about that? Funny, I'd completely forgotten until you mentioned it."

"Liar!" Nick humorously quipped. "And, of course I responded. That has to be every seventeen-year-old boy's second favorite dream. "

"I'll not ask what the first is," said Jas and immediately wished she hadn't. Nick smiled at her and Jas blushed. *So much for playing it cool.*

"Okay, you win! I must admit, it's true," Jas said. "I do think about it and you occasionally." *If only you knew.*

Then, before he could counter, Jas continued, "Well, I own my own business and have a shop on Main. *Interior Designs by Jasmine.* You may have seen it.

Zack, my husband, died five years ago of a heart attack while hunting. He was much too far from civilization to get medical help and the autopsy revealed that it would have been futile anyway."

Nick touched her arm and quietly said, "It's now my turn to convey sympathy. I'm sorry to hear of your loss. I, of course, didn't know as I was pretty much out of touch with the local happenings after moving to Albuquerque." Then Nick added, "It's beginning to look like we have a lot more in common than just Farmington High School."

Jas' heart bounced about in her chest. *Is he trying to encourage me or is he just making conversation.* "Yes, so it seems."

Nick took a drink of tea and raised his eyebrows indicating for her to continue.

Jas turned slightly in the swing, positioned one leg under her and adjusted her skirt. "Zack's years of smoking contributed to the deterioration of his health and the exertion of hunting that day was the catalyst that finally killed him." She paused momentarily apparently reflecting on the death of Zack, then continued, "After Zack died, I took some classes in interior design as I've always had a desire to do so and discovered I had a knack. I opened my own shop and, I'm happy to say, have been fairly successful."

"That's great. I'll drop by next time I'm in the vicinity."

"Wonderful! My shop is next to Penney's."

They sat in silence for a few minutes, then Nick asked, "Where do your children live?"

"Oh, we didn't have children. Not that we didn't want to. It just didn't happen. We talked about adopting but eventually decided against it."

"Oh, that's too bad." Then, attempting to get the conversation back on a lighter note, Nick asked "Jasmine is an unusual name. Is it a family name?"

"Oh no, but it just didn't come out of the blue. Sometimes don't you just have to wonder how people come up with names? My mother's favorite flower was the gardenia, however, my father strenuously objected to naming me 'Gardenia,' for which I am eternally grateful. After much discussion they agreed on 'Jasmine' since the flower is a smaller version of the gardenia and the fragrance almost identical. Not too exciting, but that's how it happened or so I've been told all my life. And you?"

"That's quite a story and bless your father for his insight. I like the name Jasmine, but may I call you Jas? Just between friends. It's less formal."

"Yes, please do, everyone does and I much prefer it." Jas responded.

"My story is not quite as interesting but a bit more logical. Would you believe I was born on Christmas Eve. However, I seriously doubt my parents named me after *Jolly Ole Saint Nick*. My complete name is Nicholas Matthew McGregor. My folks aspired to having four sons and naming us after the four apostles, Matthew, Mark, Luke and John. That's why my middle name is Matthew." They only had me. I often wondered how different my life would have been if I'd had three younger brothers. However, I'm sure when I reached my teen-years my parents were grateful they only had one." After a short pause, Nick asked, "Are you presently seeing anyone?"

Jas was caught off guard and blushed. *Is this real or is he just playing with my emotions?* A soft breeze helped ease the awkwardness surrounding the unexpected question.

Jas answered: "No, not at all. Since Zach died, I've been what you call a born-again virgin."

"Born-again virgin, that's cute, I like that. I didn't ask you if you were…."

"I know. Knee-jerk reaction. Pleading innocent and all that. It's a defense mechanism I've developed the last several years."

"Yep, that ole Catholic guilt rears its ugly head. There's no escaping it once you've been indoctrinated," Nick smiled but the smile didn't touch his eyes.

"Some things are innate and harder to discard than others. It's the concern about the fires of hell that keep me on the straight and narrow," Jas confessed.

I'M VERY ATTRACTED *to her and would like to get to know her better. She's so different from the other women I've dated. Could she be the one?* Nick noticed Jas staring at him so he said, "Hey, it's getting late. Let me drive you to your car. Where do you live anyway?"

"Actually, not too far from here but compared to this area, it's the slums."

"You're too kind and I don't believe a word of it. I'm not much of a cook but I can put a tolerable sandwich together. Will you come back tomorrow for lunch, say around noonish? Bring your swimsuit and we'll cool off in the pool before we eat. What do you think?"

"How can I refuse an offer like that? Besides, you haven't shown me the giant catfish yet."

Nick stood and jammed his hands into his pockets searching for the car keys. "Hopefully, you have a better reason for a return engagement. Believe me, I don't throw bologna and bread together for just anyone. Add a few chips and you got yourself a gourmet meal. You may be surprised at my culinary skills. Hell, even I may be surprised at my culinary skills."

Nick reached over and took her hand helping her up from the swing and led her up the driveway. He drove her back to the church parking lot. He held the door for her as she got into her car, then stood and watched as she drove away. Jas threw Nick a kiss as she slowly drove past. That little gesture would become a time honored tradition throughout the remainder of their relationship.

2
SLIGHTLY BREEZY

Rogers and Hart nailed it when they wrote *Bewitched, Bothered and Bewildered*. The lyrics could not have been more appropriate as to what she was feeling at this moment. "I'm wild again, beguiled again, a simpering, whimpering child again, bewitched, bothered and bewildered am I…" That is exactly what Jas was feeling when Nick invited her over for a day of swimming and relaxation. *Although I'm comfortable with him there's still something…MOTHER! Just leave me alone. Why don't you want me to be happy?*

Sunday loomed hot but the pool was cool and the water was dazzling reflecting the sun's rays and intensifying the blue of Jas' bright sparkling eyes. She wore a modest one-piece aqua-colored bathing suit which did justice to her five foot six, one hundred thirty-five pound athletic frame. With her medium length auburn hair pulled up in a banana clip she looked stunning.

Nick looked at her appreciatively. He also selected a modest suit foregoing the Speedo he usually wore in order to get as much tan as possible without, of course, transgressing into the realm of indecency.

After about an hour, of splashing and reminiscing school days, Nick climbed out of the pool, wrapped a towel around his waist and, smoothing back his sun-bleached hair, said, "I don't know about you, but I am starved."

Jas, shading her eyes with her hand looked up and replied, "I'm with you. Swimming, or a reasonable facsimile thereof, always makes me hungry."

Nick held out his hand and helped her out of the pool. He handed her a bright colored beach towel and said, "Hold on. I'll see what I can find," and padded toward the sliding glass doors which led to the kitchen.

Jas, smiling, sat down on the edge of the pool dangling her feet in the water. *I wish this day would never end.*

A short time later Nick reappeared. Balancing a large tray on one upturned hand, he announced, "Lunch is served." Jas rose, slipped into her sandals and sauntered in Nick's direction. He had spread a red and white checked cloth and arranged the tray on one of the patio tables situated out of the sun.

"Come sit down," he said, motioning to a comfortable looking chair.

"My, my" she exclaimed as she surveyed the assortment of meats, cheeses, crackers, fruits and vegetables artfully arranged on a bright colored platter. "Bologna sandwiches indeed. Don't tell me you did this all by yourself!"

Nick, taking the chair next to her, pretended to look hurt. He replied, "Of course I did. Just ignore the label from Abe's Deli; they try to take credit for all my creations."

They both laughed and began to eat. The day was perfect and it occurred to Jas that they were laughing a lot and genuinely enjoyed each other's company. *He is quite distinguished.* Jas surreptitiously stole glances at Nick as they ate. He had piercing blue eyes and wore his sun bleached hair in a stylish cut. His six-foot, hundred and ninety pound frame was solid for his age. The whole enchilada was wrapped in a fabulous tan.

Nick, was obviously becoming self-conscious and glanced in Jas' direction. "Is everything all right?" he asked.

Caught off-guard, Jas blushed and stuttered, "Why, why, yes. I'm enjoying the lunch very much." Then she asked, hoping to cover her rudeness at staring at him again, "Since you've retired, what else do you do to keep busy?"

Nick twisted an apple slice between his fingers. Looking thoughtful, he answered, "Oh, this place keeps me hopping, especially since my live-in maid quit."

Here he goes again. Hope he doesn't think I'm impressed with his implied comments.

Nick, oblivious to Jas' reaction each time he eluded to his prowess, went on, "I've been doing it all. I'm the chief cook, bottle washer, housekeeper and pool boy. However, I do engage a yard service. They come weekly, and," Glancing around, Nick continued, "they do a good job keeping the place looking respectable." Nick popped the apple slice into his mouth and then picked up a strawberry. Closely examining the berry, he continued, "I personally take care of the pool. I like playing in and around the water.

"And, my dear, what do you *mean* by what else do I do to keep busy?" He feigned a stern look. "I don't pick up strange women every day, if that's what you think." After a brief moment, he added, "But I would if I could… Of course, I'm just kidding. Actually I lead a pretty quiet life. Getting excited about football is about the extent of my emotional exertion."

Just kidding? Right! Jas sipped her iced tea and smiled.

"Say, I got to thinking after you came here yesterday evening that this monstrosity needs some updating. Even though there have been a few things done here and there, it's still the way my mom furnished it when I was just a kid. That's been longer than I care to remember, even if I could. How 'bout I engage you to do some cosmetic surgery on this place? Would you be interested?"

Jas, caught in the middle of taking a sip of tea, choked and coughed.

Nick jumped up, and patting her on the back, asked with concern in his voice, "Are you all right?"

Recovering from her coughing spell and trying to sound nonchalant, croaked. "I think so…went down the wrong pipe."

"Don't scare me like that!" Nick said and handed her his handkerchief.

"Thank you." Wiping tears from her eyes, Jas continued, "To answer your question, yes, I would enjoy working with you on updating your home. But, in my opinion, I think it's beautiful just the way it is. Are you sure you want to trifle with it?"

Nick looked thoughtful for a moment and then said, "Yes, I'm sure. Stephanie wasn't much of a home-body. She didn't have any desire to make the place *hers*. She was more outdoorsy and spent most of the time outside doing something-or-other. She did, however, have a green thumb. I attribute the landscaping to her talents."

Jas looked around at the lovely landscaped estate, "Really! I would have bet you had this done professionally."

Nick swept his hand around encompassing the lawn and beyond, "Stephanie's handiwork." After a moment of silent reflection, he went on to say, "Steph was also a superb cook. I had to cut way back to get down to my fighting weight after she died. I probably compensated for my loss with food for about six-months adding to the tonnage I accumulated while we were married." Nick furrowed his brow, "I am still par-anoid and watch my intake pretty closely most of the time. Once-in-awhile I succumb to the lure of ice cream. Man does not live by carrot sticks alone. So, yes, I'm ready for a change." Nick shrugged slightly. "This place feels like a mausoleum dedicated to the memory of my parents and Stephanie. There are too many ghosts roaming around."

Jas, feeling uncomfortable, repositioned herself. She crossed her legs hoping to appear more relaxed. *This place, despite its charm, is indeed a mausoleum. I constantly feel Stepha-*

nie's presence cautioning me about transgressing on her domain. I'm
flattered he wants me to update his home but…

Nick interrupted her thoughts, "I trust your judgment and expertise and know you will chase the ghosts away. What do you say?" Nick seemed to notice what appeared to be a look of confusion on Jas' face so he rushed on, "If you like, we could arrange special accommodations for my contract so as not to take you out of your shop for any appreciable length of time. I'm not opposed to evenings and weekends if that would work better for you. And I'd like to help with the painting, carpenter work and the more manly chores." Nick paused, "That is, if you agree?"

Jas sat for a long moment pondering what to do. Her head and her heart were involved in hand-to-hand combat, and in the end, heart emerged victorious. She finally said, "Okay, sounds like a deal. Evenings and weekends would work best for me." Do you have any idea what you want and how much you want to spend?"

Nick, looking around, scratched his head. "Not a clue. When we moved here from Albuquerque, I was able to convince Steph that the kitchen needed an update. She agreed. So, you wouldn't need to do anything much with the kitchen–that is, unless you think otherwise."

"Oh, I agree with you on the kitchen. The cabinets and counter tops are state of the art. I wouldn't change a thing if it were me."

"I haven't had time to think about it. The inspiration to update just occurred to me while sitting here with you. I don't want to lose the Spanish theme, but I do want to modernize the interior and get rid of the relics."

"We should do a walk-through and perhaps I can make some suggestions. Is that a comfortable place to start?" Jas queried.

"Up to you. How soon do you want to begin?"

"Well, we could do a walk-through right now…"

"Today is far too nice to think about work. I was thinking we could relax the rest of the day and then meet tomorrow evening after you close your shop. Would that be convenient?"

"Yes, in fact that would be perfect."

Nick smiled and stuck out his hand. "Then it's a deal?"

"Deal!" replied Jas, giving his hand a hearty shake.

Still holding Jas' hand, Nick pulled her up and said, "Good. C'mon. Let's go inside and watch the news on Channel 11. I'll just throw the leftovers in the frig on the way through."

ONCE INSIDE NICK ushered Jas to one of the guest bathrooms so she could shower and dress. He performed a like ritual in the master suite for himself. When they were finished, Nick built each of them another glass of ice tea and, with drinks in hand, led her to the den. They situated themselves on an oversized sofa and Nick turned on the television.

Nick glanced at Jas, and taking her hand in his, moved closer and said: "Have you thought about intimacy with anyone since your husband died?"

Jas didn't see that coming and fidgeted nervously for a moment not knowing exactly how to sidestep the question. That uncomfortable *Stephanie* feeling had resurfaced. *Now what do I do.* Finally she looked at Nick and smiled. "Of course I've thought about it. I may be old, but I'm not dead! I miss the intimacy a lot but not enough to compromise my religious convictions."

To Nick, however, her eyes said otherwise and he then slid his arm around her waist and pulled her close. She resisted a little as Nick gently elevated her chin and kissed her on the lips–tenderly at first and then passionately. His lips were warm and moist and she found herself responding in return. Jas was instantly consumed in a fiery desire that ignited her whole being. She had not felt such desire as this for a long, long time — and maybe never — at least not quite like this.

Jas' heart skipped more than a few beats and she found it difficult to breathe for a moment or two. *He wants me and I want him, but...*

She closed her eyes and before long she gave herself totally and completely to him. The afternoon slipped into evening as they lay in each other's arms, barely talking, just savoring the afterglow.

An old grandfather clock somewhere in the house chimed six times before the couple stirred. When they were dressed, Nick offered to make a light dinner and Jas, not wanting the euphoric day to end, readily accepted. Once again they sat on the patio and enjoyed the cool evening breeze as she was introduced to his modified version of the western omelet.

"You really can cook, I'm impressed."

Nick looked pleased at the complement but said, "Oh, don't be so impressed. How much talent does it take to throw a couple of eggs together with green chili, ham and cheese?"

"You haven't seen me in the kitchen."

They both endeavored to keep the conversation light not wanting to spoil the effect the love-making had on them by saying the wrong thing. Eventually, Nick asked, "You will come by tomorrow after work, won't you?"

Jas tempered the desire to say "YES! YES! YES!" and instead answered, "Sure, I planned to." Then glancing at her watch, she stood and said, "Here, I'll help with the dishes. Then I should go."

Nick stood and cupped her elbow in his hand, replying, "I'll get the dishes later. Come on, I'll see you to your car." He held the car door for her and, as she drove off down the winding drive, she blew him the now familiar kiss. He waved goodbye.

JAS, ALONE WITH her thoughts in the quiet of the night, found she was terribly conflicted between the man she *knew* she deeply loved and a lifetime of religious upbringing. She had succumbed to *the world, the flesh and the devil*, as it were. *I don't want to jeopardize my immortal soul but yet I must admit I'm hopelessly, helplessly and totally immersed in the new-found sensations of being in love and resistance and abstinence are no longer viable options. What should I do? Will I ever be forgiven? I know I need to make a decision, but not this night.*

MONDAY POUNCED LIKE a cat and Jas, having slept fitfully, groaned as she shut off the alarm squawking at her from the night stand. Thoughts of the weekend permeated her consciousness and soon she was consumed with a wealth of new-found energy. She actually leapt out of bed, showered, dressed and left for her boutique.

Jas kept herself busy dusting, rearranging accent pieces and interacting with customers. The morning passed slowly and Jas found herself constantly looking at her watch. She could scarcely wait for five o'clock to arrive and caught herself smiling as she remembered bits-and-pieces of the weekend. Bits-and-pieces, hell, every detail. Finally the little hand moved to five and the big hand moved to twelve. Jas, although eager to leave, meticulously went through her closing routine, turned off the lights and locked up. She resisted the urge to exceed the speed limit to get home. Once there and while changing into more casual attire, the telephone rang. She grabbed it up on the first ring.

"Hello."

"Well, hello yourself," Nick said.

Jas giggled. "What are you doing?"

"Waiting for you. You must be really special, I'm attempting to cook again."

Jas blinked in disbelief. *Did he actually say I must be really special.* Recovering, she replied, "I'm almost ready. Five minutes?"

"That's too long. I desperately need help. This cooking isn't as easy as the Iron Chefs lead one to believe. I've been tossing food and adding a pinch of this and a pinch of that to create what is turning out to be a complete disaster. I'm ready to throw in the towel!"

"Well, I hate to tell ya, but I'm just as inept in the kitchen as you are," Jas said through a smile.

"But not in other rooms I might add…"

"No comment. And, just for that, you're on your own in the kitchen. See you in a few."

Nick was waiting and met her at the door giving her a quick hug, "I actually missed you" he said with a smile and a slight blush.

"I actually missed you as well."

"Did you think about me today?" Nick asked.

"Only a few hundred times," Jas replied. *Dammit, wish I hadn't said that. Giving too much away?* "That is, I mean, I relived the weekend and how much fun it was."

"Well, that's not very specific." Nick responded.

"I'll have to know you better before I reveal everything including my most intimate thoughts." Now it was Jas' turn to blush.

"That's reasonable." Then after a slight pause, he asked, "Do you know me better now?"

Jas rolled her eyes in mock disgust.

Apparently, Nick noticed Jas blushing so he took her hand and pulled her further into the foyer, "Come on in and let me introduce you to a new creation. I call it La Gourmet Ala Frozen Dinner. I gave up on Pheasant Under Glass. But, take heart, my dear, there's a light at the end of the tunnel. If all else fails, at least the wine is good."

"You're too funny." Jas said as she turned and placed her shoulder bag on the table in the foyer. "La Gourmet sounds like a fine dinner. I'm sure I'll love it."

ONCE AGAIN THEY ate on the patio enjoying the evening breeze. After dinner and cleanup, Jas said, "Look, it's getting dark. The heavens have always fascinated me. You may not know it, but each year at this time, Mother Nature puts on a show."

"Come to think of it, I did see a blurb on TV about a meteor shower happening about now."

"You're right! Come on," Jas said pulling Nick by the hand back out to the patio. "Let's grab a front-row seat for the premier."

They each reclined in a deck chair situated adjacent to the pool and looked up. As twilight gradually surrendered, the dark night sky, filled with a million stars, was suddenly punctuated with a brilliant meteor display of shooting stars.

"Oh, Nick. I watch this every year. No matter how many times I've seen it, I'm always mesmerized by God's handiwork," Jas said tilting back looking towards the heavens.

"I see what you mean," Nick replied as he, too, gazed skyward. "I've never seen anything like this before. Thanks for suggesting it."

3
WHIRLWINDS

The summer slipped away and the days melted into weeks and weeks into months. Jas and Nick were soon spending virtually all their spare time together and little revolved around redecorating the mansion. Their passion for each other was almost insatiable and Jas soon lost her shyness. They both became more relaxed in each other's company and it was as though they had always been together. They had many and varied things in common including enjoying the same kind of literature, music, food and fun. They spent quiet evenings reading to each other or watching television. They found that they didn't have to make conversation; just being together was a form of communication in-and-of-itself. They shared the same sense of humor and found themselves laughing a lot over anything and everything.

By this time, Jas was completely entrenched in the relationship. She could not have been happier except that old Catholic guilt kept revisiting her in her quiet hours. Her conscience bothered her but not enough to change the pattern of satisfying her new desire. Jas often told Nick she loved him and wondered why he wouldn't say he loved her even though she knew he did. *Perhaps he's just stringing me along until the right one*

comes along? Forty-year-old bachelor syndrome? No! Go away,
Mother, he's not like that!

AS THE SUMMER faded into fall, the couple took short
weekend trips together. They often visited historic places
located in close proximity to Farmington.

"Nick, it's such a lovely day, let's take a drive up to the
Four Corners," Jas suggested. "I haven't been there since I was
a teenager."

"Me neither. Great idea! Since it only takes a little over
an hour that would be a perfect day's trip." Nick paused, "If
you're ready, we can be there by noon and grab lunch at one of
the quaint diners in the area."

"I am ready and suddenly I'm starved for a Navajo taco."

"And I know just where to get one." Nick grabbed Jas'
hand pulling her toward the door. "Come on, let's go."

As they drove toward their destination, Nick noticed Jas
had become thoughtful. He said, "You seem preoccupied. Are
you all right, honey?"

"What? Oh, yes, I'm fine. I was just wondering if the ter-
ritory was divided purposefully to form the perfect square
where the four states meet, or if that happened by accident,"
she mused.

"Not likely accidental and I don't think it was purposefully engineered. That would take a heap of surveying," Nick
chirped. "The story I heard was that the Four Corners area
belonged to Mexico until the mid-1800s. After years of fighting
over that hunk of desert, finally some civic minded individu-
als suggested a cement pad be poured designating the bound-
aries. The idea was embraced and the slab was poured. It was
scored into four equal sections forming what we know as the
Four Corners thus making New Mexico, Arizona, Utah and
Colorado blood borders."

Jas chuckled, "That's clever—blood borders. Didn't know you were such a historian."

"Why, thank you, my sweet. I'm glad you appreciate my cleverness." Nick smiled, obviously pleased with himself.

Nick, living up to his promise, pulled into the parking lot of a small dive of a restaurant. Jas raised her eyebrows as she surveyed the establishment.

"Come on, live dangerously," Nick teased as he opened her door.

Much to Jas' surprise, the interior was clean and nostalgic. She was served the best Navajo tacos she had ever eaten.

After lunch, they drove up to the monument and walked out onto the slab of cement. Since the sun was directly overhead, there were no distorting shadows as they each placed a foot in a different state and joined hands. Thus, they concluded they were in all four states at the same time. Standing there, Jas looked around over her shoulder and remarked, "When I came here with my parents as a teen, I was agile enough to place my hands and feet in all four states. You know, it's just something tourists have to do." Then smiling at the memory, she added, "Mom said I looked like a turtle."

"Show me!" Nick teased.

"Not unless you want to take me home in traction."

A passing fellow visitor held up his camera and offered to take a polaroid of them.

Later, when Jas examined the photo more closely, she reflected on how happy and content they looked. She was inspired to start a photo album arranging, in chronological order, the pictures of the two of them she'd been collecting.

THAT SAME AFTERNOON on the way home, as they passed through Aztec, Jas suggested they stop at the Aztec Ruins National Monument which was located just a few miles from Farmington.

"That's a great idea. Since it's still early, we'll have plenty of time to explore the ancient mysteries. We, Stephanie and I that is, came here on a couple of occasions. However, we only brought the girls once. They were not in the least amused," Nick said.

"Guess old Indian stuff and mummies doesn't interest teens," Jas responded. "Zach wasn't much into it either so the only time we came was when we had company that asked to visit the ruins."

"Well, we're here now. Looks like we have an hour or so before closing," Nick said pointing to the sign advertising visitor hours were from 8:00 a.m. to 5:00 p.m. seven days a week.

Nick and Jas spent an hour wandering through the antiquated catacombs dating back from the 11th to the 13th centuries. In concert with her new hobby, the photo album, Jas approached a young couple and asked if they would take a picture of Nick and her with the camera she had purchased at the gift shop. This was another tradition that would continue throughout their relationship. The album was the thing Jas treasured most as it was a history of their lives together. She kept it on the nightstand closest to her bed and examined it every night before falling asleep.

FALL RELUCTANTLY WOULD soon be a memory as winter stood waiting in the proscenium. However, before the snow and cold completely took over, Nick suggested they take the narrow gauge to Silverton.

"Nick! The coveted Silverton narrow gauge train ride?" Jas squealed. "I don't know what to say."

"How 'bout happy anniversary. Today marks three months together."

"You remembered!" Although three months wasn't a milestone by any stretch, still Jas was moved. Tears formed in her eyes and she pressed her face against Nick's chest lest he see she was crying.

Nick wasn't that easily fooled; he lifted her chin and kissed her gently on the lips.

THE DAY WAS pleasant and the hour's drive from Farmington to Durango, the point of departure, was breath-taking, especially during this time of year. The passenger cars were painted bright yellow and the jet black engine was fueled by coal. It was purported to be one that was used in the late 1800s. The round trip from Durango to Silverton took approximately three and one-half hours not including the hour layover in Silverton allowing passengers to have lunch and wonder about exploring the historic town.

"I don't think we'll have a lot of competition this late in the season," Nick said when they arrived in Durango. However, when they approached the depot, Nick was surprised at the number of vehicles in the parking lot. He pulled up in front of the station and let Jas out at the entrance. He patted his shirt pocket and then said, "I have our tickets. Believe it or not, I was smart enough to get them online. Honey, you go on in while I find a place to park."

Jas, waiting in the terminal, anxiously looked around for Nick when the conductor shouted, "ALL ABOARD." Turning her head left and right hoping to see him, she was near panic when she heard his voice from behind her, "We better get going." He put his arm around her waist and hustled her toward the boarding platform.

Once aboard, the couple settled into their seats and watched from a window as the train chugged up the mountain climbing toward Silverton. They were now out of the desert and into tall pines. The aspen trees were a sight to behold having been transformed by the autumn frost to brilliant gold as they stood in groves snuggled in among the green pines, surrounded by the reds, oranges and yellows of the oak brush. The La Plata's snow-capped peaks could be seen in the distance adding more enchantment to the wonderful virgin landscape.

The train stopped at the station and passengers began to disembark. Upon arrival, they found Silverton still teaming with tourists despite the weather turning colder. Nick took Jas' hand, helping her down the steps to the platform, and asked, "What sounds good for lunch?"

Jas looked around as she zipped up her blazer and replied, "There used to be the most charming Mexican restaurant just a few blocks from here. Let's see if we can find it."

"Hell yes! I love Mexican food and I'm starved."

Pulling on her leather gloves, Jas replied, "Okay cowboy. Let's roll."

The Hacienda was exactly where Jas remembered it being. Although the restaurant was crowded, the couple didn't have to wait long for a table. They ordered the daily special which consisted of tamales, tacos and refried beans. Their lunch was served within minutes. Apparently, *The Hacienda* accommodated the train passengers knowing they had limited time for a meal.

"This is the best Mexican food I've ever had," Nick managed to sputter through a mouthful of tamale. "I'm glad you remembered this place."

Jas bobbed and nodded in agreement while stuffing the remains of a taco into her mouth.

Nick's eyes twinkled and he smiled broadly as he said, "After we finish, I want to take you to one of *my* favorite places." Jas, furrowed her brow, and dabbing her mouth with a napkin, replied, "Okay, I'm finished." Then she added, "I know that look. You're up to something. Out with it, what is it?"

"Patience, my dear," Nick commented as he perused the check. He extracted his wallet from his rear pocket, took out a twenty and left it anchored under the candle centerpiece on the table. Then standing, he tucked Jas' arm under his and ushered her out the door and up the street to a little shop a few doors from *The Hacienda*.

A TINY BELL above the door tinkled when they entered the *Wampum,* a quaint little shop featuring handmade jewelry. The pleasant aroma of cinnamon permeated the air and Jas looked around overwhelmed at the array of authentic Indian jewelry. She was drawn to a glass showcase displaying pieces made by a local Native American artist, Grandma Corn Blossom. Jas recognized the name as Grandma Corn Blossom's jewelry was well known throughout the Southwest.

"Oh, look Nick. These were made by Corn Blossom," Jas said grabbing Nick's arm and pointing to the display.

Nick was way ahead of her and had already selected a fetish necklace. It was fashioned of tiny multi-colored birds carved out of semi-precious materials such as red cornelian, tan jasper, rose quartz, green malachite, black onyx, and natural turquoise strung on a sterling silver chain, interspaced with small brown Indian beads and secured with a sterling silver clasp.

He held it up to the light and turned it over and back again performing a closer inspection of the fetish bird beads. When he was satisfied that the quality was as expected, Nick handed a hundred dollar bill to the clerk. Jas stood in wide-eyed amazement watching the exchange.

"No need to wrap it," Nick smiled.

Accepting the bill, the clerk turned and said, "I'll be back momentarily with your change, Sir."

"No, you keep the change." Nick said as he stepped behind Jas and gently fastened the piece around her neck.

"Nick, What a nice surprise, thank you." Jas then stood on her tiptoes and examined herself in the large mirror behind the counter adjusting the tiny bird beads. "I'm…"

Before she could finish, the clerk was back. "Thank you, Sir, for your generously," he said as he placed several bills in his shirt pocket.

"You're welcome." Then looking at the clerk over Jas' shoulder, Nick asked, "By the way, what's your name?"

"I'm known as Wapi."

"Well, Wapi," Nick said, leaning his forearms on the counter, "I've heard there's a legend..."

Wapi was quick to respond obviously eager to relate the story. He straightened his shoulders and answered, "Indeed there is, Sir."

Nick looked at Jas and raised his eyebrows. He then made small circles with his hands gesturing for Wapi to continue. Jas appeared to be captivated by what was transpiring. *A real Indian legend?*

Wapi stood behind the counter and placing his hands on the glass counter top, looked skyward for a moment as though he were praying. He then took a deep breath and related the Indian legend.

"My people believe the fetish has magical power to protect and aid its owner." Wapi nodded toward Jas. "That would be you." Her hand went immediately to the necklace and she caressed it. Wapi continued, "Fetishes are regarded with superstition, extravagant trust, reverence and obsessive devotion." Still looking at Jas, he leaned closer as if sharing a secret and continued, "Guard it well or you may incur the wrath of the Kachinas who are touted to be deified ancestral spirits and have been known to visit pueblos at intervals."

Nick and Jas remained still for a few moments in silent reflection. Nick finally said, "Umm, thank you, Wapi. You weave quite a fascinating tale."

"Pardon me, Sir," Wapi said, somewhat indignant. "My rendition was told exactly as it was handed down to me through the generations. My people carefully guard their inheritance."

"Oh, yes, I do believe that." Nick bowed his head, "I apologize as I meant no disrespect." He then took Jas' hand. "So, my dear, you now have a powerful talisman in your possession. Be careful not to anger the Kachinas."

Jas, having been thoroughly intrigued by the rendition, was still absorbing its meaning. Not only was this the first gift Nick had given her, but it possessed mystical powers as well. To her, it would always be considered sacred and for more noble reasons. *I will treasure this forever.*

Nick paused at the door as they were leaving and turned back, "Wapi, I'm curious. Just exactly what does your name mean in English?"

Wapi smiled broadly and, retrieving the generous tip Nick had given him from his shirt pocket, he said, "It translates to Lucky in your language—really!"

Nick just shook his head as he held the door open for Jas.

HAVING ALREADY LOST her heart, Jas became even more entangled in the relationship. She had never known anyone quite like Nick. He was everything she ever dreamed of. She felt she had loved him, or the idea of him, her whole life. What's that old saying: "What he doesn't have, he doesn't need."

4
CLOUDY SKIES

Nick was preoccupied with his new found love and the update on his mansion seemed to have been put on the back burner. Jas, however, was eager to begin and kept urging Nick to start the project. One afternoon Jas suggested they visit some of Farmington's furniture stores to get an idea of what was available. Farmington, being located in the Southwest, was saturated with high-end shops featuring Southwestern design.

As they went from store-to-store, Jas would take notes and if Nick liked a particular design or style, she recorded the name of the artisan and later explored the cost of a custom-made replica usually with some desired modification. Although no artisan was ever commissioned, it was fun nonetheless to daydream. When Nick saw an item he liked that was in stock, he would always look to Jas for approval before purchasing it. She would then shake her head–not always up and down.

And, as if he needed to further prove his lack of style, Nick suggested they apply terra cotta paint throughout the mansion stating it would give the home an authentic Southwestern flavor. A stunned Jas faked a gag.

"Nick, tell me you're not serious. If you paint all the rooms terra cotta, they will be considerably darker and you'll lose a lot of the rustic charm that was built in at the time of construction."

Nick raised his hands in a defensive motion, "That's why I hired you. I know my shortcomings. I surrender. You're the visionary. From this point forward I'm your minion and will follow your lead."

Jas softened when she realized she had hurt his feelings. "I do want your input. After all, you have to live here. However, I'm not going to let you make drastic mistakes that you will later regret."

Nick smiled and said, "You're driving this bus. Go ahead and do what you were trained to do. I'm sure I'll love it."

NICK'S FATHER HAD been infatuated with Kachina dolls and native pottery. Over the years he had amassed a considerable, not to mention valuable, collection of both. He had a version, or two, of nearly every Kachina imaginable, some of his favorites were *Eagle Dancer, Mother Crow* and *Hoop Dancer.* However, his very favorite was *Story Teller.*

Mr. McGregor's pottery was estimated to be worth thousands of dollars. Without exception, all of the items were extremely valuable having been purchased many years before and were increasing in value with the passage of time. Nick had them displayed helter-skelter throughout the house which made them vulnerable to impending disaster not to mention they were not displayed to be ascetically pleasing. Jas, wanting to honor Nick's father's collection and protect the pieces from getting damaged said, "Nick, I think if we have a special display case built with glass doors all of the treasures could be kept safely in one place and yet visible. What do you think?"

"What a great idea. Why hadn't I thought of that?"

Jas smiled. *Maybe he'll realize now how much he needs me.*

"You know, I think I can construct the display case. I'm pretty handy when it comes to woodworking, especially book-shelves and display pieces."

"Excellent! You having made it will make it even more special."

Nick had a shop in his over-sized three-car garage that would be the envy of every carpenter. He immediately set to work on the project and had it completed and installed with-in two weeks. When he had finished, he told Jas, "Close your eyes. I have a surprise," He then took her hand and led her to the recreation room.

"Okay, open!"

When Jas saw the finished product she squealed with delight. "Nick! It's beautiful and exactly what I envisioned."

Nick was a perfectionist or better described as obsessive/compulsive. The display case was made from oak and etched with Southwest designs in the wood on the top brace. It was from floor to ceiling and encompassed the entire breadth of one wall. Even at that, it was barely adequate enough to hold all the items.

Helping Nick transfer his collections to the bookcase was great fun. Jas would stop once-in-awhile to appreciate the workmanship that went into making the Kachina dolls. She mentally selected her favorite and fingered it lovingly. It was, of course, the *Story Teller*. The main character was a happy, chubby Indian, the story teller, and lots of children were depict-ed climbing all over her. They all were laughing and having great fun. It made her happy; it was an uplifting piece. Happy and loving–not the way she remembered her own childhood when she and her sister would listen to wild and sometimes morbid bedtime stories their father told usually when he was drunk and abusive.

Then there were the fights her parents would have over him being away from home days on end and coming home with the tell-tail signs of having been with another woman.

Her mother had done her best to protect her daughters–even through the times when their father would disappear for days and then come home with flimsy excuses about where he had been. Those days had left their impression. That was certain! Even as a child of tender years, Jas was taught by her mother not to trust men. She could still hear her mother say, *They will only use you, abuse you and discard you when they are through with you.*

Jas loved her parents in spite of it all, but she closed off a portion of her heart that had never been open by anyone–not even her late husband. Standing there, she gently stroked the merry little Kachina as a tear slid down her cheek. Suddenly, Nick breezed into the room.

"Hey, are you still among the living?" he asked.

Jas held up the Kachina. "Oh, I'm just wondering what story is being told to cause so much joy in all these little children. This is truly lovely. Something about it has captivated my heart. We have to find a very special place for this piece."

UPDATE ON THE mansion was progressing and the results of every project were impressive. The easy way with which they worked together had not gone unnoticed by either of them. Each day they grew a little closer; a bit more comfortable. There were times Jas would look at Nick as they were working, and suddenly be overcome by this strange and terrifying feeling. That little door that harbored her deepest self was slowly being pried open. Nobody but Nick had ever been allowed that close. Her mother's voice continued to echo in her mind, warning her again-and-again not to trust.

It didn't help matters that one of Nick's traits was that he liked to banter and tease. It appeared that he thoroughly enjoyed graphic descriptions of encounters with, what he described as beautiful women at the bank, grocery store, or wherever he happened to be. His intent was nothing more than

to elicit a reaction from Jas. Nick put a lot of credence in jeal-
ousy. His theory was, if you weren't jealous, you really didn't
care much. Jas played along, but inside a feeling clenched at
her gut that made her want to run away. Her mother's voice
shrieked ever louder in her ears.

The taunting began as harmless banter meant in fun, but a
little feeling of suspicion suddenly took shape in Jas' mind —
something black and foreboding. In the heat of passion and the
warmth and comfort of the relationship they had built, she
never considered the possibility that Nick might betray her.
Now she wasn't so sure. She began to feel insecure and even
threatened by these other *beautiful* women whom she had never met. The black form she had created in her mind urged her
to face herself in the mirror. She stared at the reflection with
judgment and loathing convincing herself she could never
measure up to these voluptuous ghosts that haunted her thinking. *A happy and satisfied man does not continue to shop.* She would
not make the same mistake her mother made. Infidelity was
not something she could or would ever tolerate.

DAYS, WEEKS AND months slid by and the holidays were
upon them. Nicole, Nick's daughter who lived in Farmington,
called and invited Nick for Thanksgiving dinner. Nicole was
well aware that Nick was seeing someone so she said, "Dad, I
have a bird big enough to feed an army. If you like, you're welcome to bring someone."

After a few moments, Nick replied, "That's very nice of
you, Nicole. I will."

"Wonderful! Let's plan to dine around two."

"We'll be there." Then, almost as an afterthought, Nick
asked, "Can we bring something?"

"No, but thanks for offering. Mother taught me well and,
believe it or not, I have this gig under control."

Nick laughed, "I'll just bet you do, Sweetie. See you Thursday."

AS SOON AS he hung up the phone, Nick called Jas, "Hey, you! Guess what? We've been invited to Nicole's for Thanksgiving."

"We? You and me?" Jas wasn't sure what he meant.

"Yes, silly, you and me. You'll love the grandkids..."

Jas didn't hear the rest of what he was saying. She was too excited about being included in *his* family's celebration.

"Hey, you still there?" Nick asked.

"Yes, yes, I'm here."

"So what do you think?"

"I'd love to meet them..."

"Okay then. Nicole said two o'clock Thursday."

"Should I bring something like pumpkin pie?"

"No, but I did remember my manners and asked but Nicole said she has the dinner all planned." Then Nick added, "We'll take some wine."

JEREMY AND NICOLE were warm and friendly and Jas was treated like a member of the family. Nick's grandchildren were enthusiastic, energetic and extremely excited anticipating Christmas which was right around the corner. Much to Jas' delight, they immediately bonded and clung to her as though she was a new-found grandmother. They even argued over who would sit by her at dinner.

Jas teased Nick, "Look, I have a fan club."

"Yeah, I noticed. They never fought over who would sit by me." Nick teased back. "I'm jealous!"

Everyone had congregated in the kitchen and soon Jeremy said, "It's pretty crowded in here, Nick. Let's go catch the end of the game."

Jas and Nicole became fast friends. Although Jas was old enough to be Nicole's mother, she looked young enough to be a contemporary. The two women engaged in relaxed conversation as Jas assisted Nicole in the dinner preparation.

"I really love what you are doing with the villa," Nicole said as she gently mixed a fruit salad. It's great to see Dad act alive again instead of doing nothing but managing his investments. How boring!"

Jas rolled her eyes in agreement. Then she said, "You know, that project is my dream job."

Nicole smiled, "That's great. I grew to love the estate but it wasn't always that way."

"Really! Why not?" Jas inquired.

"Well, we, that is my sisters and I, weren't too happy about leaving Albuquerque. We resisted the move to Farmington. Leaving life-long friends and moving to a hick town was inconceivable."

"I can only imagine..." Jas interjected.

Nicole nodded, "And to make it worse, we moved over the Christmas holidays. I think we made Dad's life hell for a while. He probably looked forward to the international trips to get away from us."

Jas, leaning against the kitchen counter and replied, "Moving is always emotional but especially for teens."

"Right!" Nicole asked and pointed to the oven, "Would you check the sweet potato casserole?"

Jas looked around, "Potholders?"

"In the top drawer...over there." Then Nicole continued with her rendition, "However, when we gave it a chance, we learned the hick town really wasn't so bad after all. We eventually forgave Dad for uprooting us. The move proved to be a blessing in disguise."

"I've always thought Farmington was a great place to live," Jas agreed as she peered into the oven. "I think the casserole is ready. The marshmallows are golden brown."

"Yipps. Would you take it out?" Nicole asked as she put the finishing touches on a relish tray.

"It smells heavenly," Jas remarked pulling the casserole from the oven.

"Thank you, Jas. It's my mother's recipe," Nicole said as she continued to arrange the relish tray. "I hope you get to meet my sister, Theresa. She is much like Dad, always joking and teasing. They *love* watching people squirm! One of these days," Nicole predicted, "the shoe will be on the other foot. I want to be there when that happens."

"I am all too familiar with your dad's teasing."

"I'm sure you are. No one escapes Dad's wrath." Nicole smiled pleasantly and poured gravy into a gravy boat. She then picked up a beautifully arranged platter of food, and looking around, said, "I think we're ready to eat. Would you mind bringing the fruit salad and gravy?"

Jas scooped up the items and followed Nicole into the dining room which the grandchildren had decorated with purple turkeys, orange pumpkins and antiquated pilgrims appended to the sliding glass door. A cornucopia centerpiece of silk fall flowers, dried ears of corn and terra cotta colored candles complimented the table setting.

Everyone was seated and the room became quiet as Jeremy folded his hands in his lap. He looked around in what appeared to Jas to be love and appreciation. His gaze then fell upon Nick, "Nick, I believe this year it's your turn to say grace. Will you do the honors?"

"It would be my pleasure," Nick said as he made the sign of the cross and bowed his head in prayer. "Bless us, Oh Lord, and these thy gifts which we are about to receive from thy bounty through Christ our Lord." Nick paused and looked at each family member seated at the table. "And thank you God, for my family, those that are present and those that are not. Please continue to keep us sheltered within your divine protection." He then picked up his napkin and placed it on his lap indicating he had finished. When he looked up, he saw a hurt look on Jas' face. He hurriedly added, "Also, Heavenly Father, I'm grateful to have been blessed with good friends to help me along life's journey," and reaching over squeezed Jas' hand.

THE ATMOSPHERE WAS light and happy as they shared a scrumptious turkey dinner with all the trimmings. The dessert choices were pumpkin, pecan or apple pie *ala mode*. Nick sampled a slice of each.

Jas helped with the clean-up and afterwards everyone settled in the living room. The McGregor family, all accomplished musicians, took turns playing the piano. When everyone had taken a turn, Jeremy asked, "How 'bout you, Jas. Do you play?"

"Well, not…" Jas started to reply.

"Oh, come on. You can peck something out," Nick coaxed. "We're all amateurs. Give it a try."

Okay, you asked for it. Jas timidly walked to the piano and sat down. When she began to play she surprised everyone, most especially Nick. She played her all-time favorite, Gershwin's *Rhapsody in Blue.*

After she finished an almost perfect rendition, an astounded Nick said, "You're just full of surprises, aren't you?"

She smiled coyly, "If you only knew."

Nick raised his eyebrows in mock exaggeration and feigning understanding, just nodded his head.

"Actually," Jas confessed "I studied piano for years. Music has been a big part of my life and has helped me through some pretty tough times.

"You may remember, a few years back when the United States hosted the summer Olympics, a tribute was made to Gershwin. Part of the entertainment consisted of a multitude of pianos, all painted sky-blue, placed at different levels on the stage. The pianists, sporting sky-blue tuxedos and formal dresses, played *Rhapsody in Blue* in perfect unison. I was awestruck. It was so beautiful; I could have kicked myself for not recording it, but who knew?

"Afterwards, I bought the sheet music and practiced until I had the refrain committed to memory. I'm certainly not skilled enough to play all of the intricate parts of that magnificent composition. However, I can now play the refrain from memory and often do so at home to keep my skills honed. Thought I'd better fess up before you asked me to play Chopin or Beethoven."

"I'm still impressed," Nick responded, "you certainly nailed it." *What an amazing creature she is. Who does that? Who in the hell does that?*

5
COLD FRONT

Although Farmington is situated in the desert, the winters can get cold. This winter was no exception; the weatherman predicted there would be a white Christmas if the current conditions prevailed. Living alone and not having space to go all out, Jas limited her holiday decorating. She carefully placed her heirloom Llardo nativity set on the fireplace mantel, added an evergreen wreath to the front door and positioned a small, sparsely trimmed tree in front of the living room window. Traditionally, she did, however, make sure to have an elaborately decorated tree on display in her shop.

NICK'S DAUGHTER, THERESA, planned to travel to Farmington from Santa Fe with her family to spend the week before Christmas with her father and Nicole, a time when all the children would be on Christmas break.

Nicole looked relieved when Nick suggested that Theresa and her family stay with him at the villa because of Nicole's limited space. "Thank you, Dad. That takes a load off of my mind. I've been juggling kids trying to figure out how to accommodate our visitors."

"I'm happy to do it, Nicole. Plus, I'll get to spend a lot more time with the Pearson family."

"Yep, the kids will love that." Then after a pause, Nicole furrowed her brow and added, "Please don't let them talk you into taking them for a ride in the plane. The weather is too unpredictable."

"Whoa, no worries there, little girl. I don't fly unless there's a sun in the sky. Remember what happened when I took your brood for a ride and the weather got rough?"

"Ouch! Did you have to bring that up." Nicole, cringing at the memory, said, "Wrong choice of words, huh?"

NICK TOLD JAS of the upcoming visit and asked her if she would help him.

"I haven't had the heart to put the Christmas stuff out since Stephanie died. And frankly I wouldn't know where to begin." Nick scratched at the stubble on his chin apparently reflecting on the past. "Steph and the girls always took care of the decorating. My participation was to procure a tree and put the outside lights up."

"Oh, Nick, of course I'll help," Jas replied, hoping she didn't appear too eager.

"You really are a love, you know."

Jas beamed. Then she rushed on, "I have some current items in the shop we could use and…"

Nick held his hand up. "Honey, as if you don't do enough, I have another favor to ask."

Jas noticed the anxiety in his voice. "Sure, what is it?"

Nick then blurted, "I need help with the meals, too! That is, if you're willing. I'm so inadequate in the kitchen. You've seen my skills; they're pretty embarrassing. I don't want my company to live on western omelets the whole week."

Is he actually pulling me into his family circle or am I just a substitute for the departed live-in maid? Jas crossed her arms and leaned forward on the table, "Aren't you forgetting something?"

"Probably, but what are you referring to?"

"My culinary skills, for example."

"Oh, damn! That's right." Nick rubbed his forehead looking thoughtful, then he replied, "Okay, you make a good point. What we'll do is buy everything we can at the deli and spruce the meals up with salads, relishes, desserts and whatever else you think we need."

"Wonderful idea! We can probably pull that off. You know I'm happy to assist wherever I can," Jas said and meant it with all her heart.

"I appreciate you more than you know. Besides, your involvement will give you the opportunity to get to know Theresa."

Maybe I've misjudged him… Go away, Mother. Quit making me doubt the man I love.

THERESA'S VISIT WAS twofold unbeknownst to Nick. The sisters had secretly planned a surprise birthday party for him the Saturday before Christmas which was not his actual Christmas Eve birthday but worked in nicely with the weekend. Nicole recruited Jas to help pull off the surprise.

The afternoon of the party the women enlisted Nick to babysit while they went on a feigned shopping trip. The deception allowed them to slip away and surreptitiously decorate the dining room at The River Side, Nick's favorite restaurant. Nicole and Theresa, on the sly, invited all of their relatives and friends and swore them to secrecy. Unfortunately, Nick's other two daughters were unable to attend, but they promised to call.

Upon arriving at the restaurant, the conspirators began stringing baby blue and white, Nick's favorite color combination, crepe paper swags from the ceiling.

"Come on, Jas," Nicole said. "Help me fill these damn bal-loons. They keep floating away before I can get them tied."

Jas aborted spreading the linen table cloths and went to assist Nicole. They soon had a supply of balloons to place strategically throughout the venue.

Theresa took over where Jas left off. Each of the six tables was decorated with a center piece consisting of white carnations accented with blue Christmas balls and blue satin ribbons. When they finished, they stood back and admired their handiwork.

Nicole put her hands on her hips and, looking around, said, "Looks like our work is done here."

"It looks great! Nick will be so surprised," Jas added. They high-fived all around and left to get ready for the evening.

THE EUPHORIC ATMOSPHERE convinced Jas she need-ed a new dress for the occasion. Time was running out so she went first to an exclusive boutique where she found exactly what she wanted. The dress was blue, of course, and wildly expensive. But Jas decided it was worth it. The dress compli-mented Jas' figure and was remarkably attractive. Standing before the three-way mirror in the changing area, Jas examined herself and then stepped out of the dressing room to where the clerk waited.

"What do you think?" Jas asked as she pirouetted.

Looking Jas over as she modeled the dress, the clerk said, "It's lovely; it was made for you." Then she pointed to Jas' feet. "We have a pair of matching shoes which you really should have to complete the Cinderella-look."

Jas agreed, "…as long as they're not made of glass," she teased.

AT THE APPOINTED hour, the invited guests, including Jas, congregated in the dining room of the restaurant anticipating the arrival of the guest of honor. They didn't have to wait long. Nick, flanked on each side by his two amazingly beautiful daughters, was caught totally off guard. As they entered, the crowd roared "SURPRISE." The look on Nick's face was priceless. When he recovered, he turned to his daughters and, admonishing them, said "I could have had a heart attack, you know!" and he kissed them each on the cheek. Almost immediately, the guests gathered around him wishing him a happy birthday. Some of his male friends stepped in to rescue him and whisked him off to the bar to partake in liquid refreshment.

"Don't be long," Nicole shouted as they left, "dinner will be served in fifteen minutes."

Nick gave her an acknowledging wave of the hand as the noisy group of men ushered him hastily into the adjoining bar.

Nicole just shook her head in mock disgust.

The hostesses busied themselves greeting and seating the other guests. Theresa placed Nicole and herself on each side of Nick at the head table. She designated Jas to be seated at one of the front tables along with some of the McGregor relatives, including two of Nick's aunts.

The rest of the tables were left open for whoever wanted to sit together. The aunts, both in their eighties, were very chatty and witty dinner companions. They played off of each other and, in the short time they sat together during dinner, Jas learned more of Nick's childhood than she had from Nick the whole time they had been together.

Looking up and appearing to search her memory, Aunt Mary said, "I remember that Nick was a star athlete in high school."

Aunt Frances interrupted by adding, "Yep, and always in the emergency room with some kind injury."

"His poor mother," Aunt Mary said. "I went to the hospital with her the time he had three ribs broken playing football." Then she paused and, adjusting her shawl around her shoulders, smugly added, "Louise confided in *me* that she was happy he was an only child."

Aunt Frances rolled her eyes. "Yes, of course, Mary," she replied as she slid her chair back and crossed her legs. Looking pretty defiant, she continued, "You always were the first to know anything. Wonder how the newspaper stayed in business with that kind of competition."

Oh, my God. Am I going to have to referee an eighty-year-old cat fight?

Just then the photographer appeared. He had been engaged to take pictures to commemorate the celebration. *Saved!* "Come on, ladies. Put your arms around each other and smile pretty for the camera," Jas coaxed. The sisters complied and soon they were happily conversing as if nothing had happened. Jas was relieved. *That's sisters for you.*

Nick and the others hadn't reappeared when the waiters began serving steaming plates of food. Nicole whispered to Theresa, "Do you think I should go get them?" Theresa looked perplexed and shrugged her shoulders apparently not knowing what to do about retrieving the guest of honor. Finally, looking disgusted, Theresa slammed her napkin down on the table and shoved her chair back. "I'll go!" she snapped. Before she could rise, she looked up and saw Nick and his entourage returning to the dining room. She nodded to Nicole and both girls heaved a sigh of relief.

Jas observed the daughters' interaction. *Good grief! First the aunts and now this. I hope and pray nothing happens to spoil this event.*

THE DINING ROOM grew quiet when Uncle Theo clinked a knife against his glass and rose to give the invocation.

"We are gathered here to honor our beloved Nicholas Matthew McGregor on his sixtieth birthday." Uncle Theo then raised his glass and continued, "Nick, may the Lord bless you and keep you; may He make His face shine upon you and be gracious unto you; may He turn His face toward you and give you peace and," Theo paused, smiled and looked around the room, "may he give you at least sixty more years to figure it all out."

"Hear, hear," rumbled throughout the venue as everyone rose, raised their glass and drank to Nick.

THERE WAS A pleasant hum of conversation, clinking of silverware and ripples of laughter as guests plowed through their dinner. When it looked as though the guests had finished the main course, Nicole stopped the waiter that was removing dinnerware from the head table and whispered to him. He nodded his head and disappeared into the kitchen. Then, as though it were the final act of a Broadway production, the band struck up Happy Birthday. Suddenly, the door between the kitchen and dining room burst open and the wait staff wheeled in a massive birthday cake on a serving cart with all sixty candles ablaze.

"Oh, my God," Nick muttered and rested his forehead on his hand.

The guests stood and clapped and cheered as Nick's daughters dragged him from his chair over to where the cake had been positioned and urged him to blow out the candles.

"Come on, Dad. You can do it!" Nicole said and gently pushed him forward.

"I don't know. Looks pretty much like a forest fire to me," Nick said winking at her.

"Hurry, Dad." Theresa jabbed him in the side. "The candles are melting."

Nick then took a deep breath and blew.

In one breath, all of the candles were extinguished. Nick, looking pleased with himself, grabbed his chest and feigning a faint, weakly uttered, "I did it, by George, I did it." He looked at Jas who gave him a thumbs-up. Everyone laughed and applauded as the waiters took over and began cutting and serving cake and ice cream.

As the last of the cake was distributed, the band began playing *Can't Live Without You.* The song was Jas' favorite Carroll Multz composition. She began to sway her head in rhythm with the music. Nick's eyes captured hers and he immediately dabbed his mouth with a napkin and excused himself from his table. Nick kept her in his gaze as he approached her table. Extending his right hand, he asked, "Lovely lady, may I have this dance?"

Her eyes never left his as she rose to her feet. Others were already moving in rhythm to the sweet band sounds as Nick and Jas stepped onto the dance floor. As Nick held Jas in his arms, he noticed how lovely she looked.

"You look amazing, my love," he whispered.

She smiled, feeling the warmth of his body as they began to glide to the music. They made a handsome couple and the other guests stopped dancing to watch. This delighted Nick as he loved being the center of attention. He began to show off and, in his best Fred Astaire/Ginger Rogers imitation, led Jas around the floor. Jas did her best to keep up but his twists, turns and dips soon made her dizzy. *If I faint or fall down, I'll just die.* She felt self-conscious and could hardly wait for the dance to end. At its conclusion, as Nick escorted her back to her table, Jas closed her eyes and silently thanked God for helping her through the ordeal without incident.

"You're a good dancer," he said.

"I'm not so sure, I suddenly feel queasy."

Nick held her chair for her but before leaving, he squeezed her hand transmitting a longing and a desire to be intimate. Jas sat down, blushing at what she was thinking.

Nick moved back to his table and danced with each of his daughters. He then went from table to table visiting with friends and family. He even managed to dance with all the female guests including his eighty-year-old aunts. Jas watched as Nick socialized but was relieved he had other dancing partners. Several male attendees invited her to dance but she begged off using new shoes as an excuse.

One obviously intoxicated, over-zealous cousin of Nick's said, "Take the damn things off and come on and cut a rug with me!"

At that moment and to Jas' relief, Aunt Mary intervened, "JACK! As usual, you're acting like an ass." Then Aunt Mary, obviously pleased with her play on words, elbowed Aunt Francis, "His mother named him appropriately, jackass!" Then to Jack she scolded, "Get on now, go sit down."

Around eleven the party finally dwindled down to just a few couples. When Nick said his last farewells to the stragglers, he sauntered over to Jas' table and sat down by her. He slid his arm around her waist and took her hand saying, "Theresa and her family are staying at the villa, so unfortunately, I won't be able to see you tonight."

"I know…"

Nick gently squeezed her hand, "Will you come have dinner with me tomorrow evening after they leave?"

"Of course, I'd be delighted to join you for dinner." Jas squeezed back and continued, "I hope you enjoyed yourself. The girls worked so hard putting this gig together. They are truly wonderful, Nick. Do you know how lucky you are to have such lovely daughters?"

"I did enjoy myself. In fact, I had a blast. Just call me Wapi. I *do* know how lucky I am and not just because of lovely daughters."

Jas laughed remembering the encounter with Wapi at the *Wampum* in Silverton. She also knew he had included her in his last comment.

"This was so totally unexpected and you made it even more special," Nick said and furrowed his brow. "How did you manage to keep this a secret from me, you traitor?" he teased.

Nick noticed the smug look on Jas' face as she replied, "I was sworn to secrecy. I didn't want to alienate your daughters by letting the cat out of the bag."

"I see. So, you'd rather alienate me?"

"Yep!"

"Geez, woman."

At that moment Theresa joined them "What's Dad geezing women about now?"

ALMOST AS FAST as it began, the party was over. When everyone had left, Nick walked Jas to her car. He softly kissed her lips. How she wanted to be with him tonight—to feel the warmth and touch of his body close to hers. All the way home *Can't Live Without You* played and replayed in her head.

Jas sighed as she closed the door behind her. She kicked off her stilettoes in the foyer and headed toward the bedroom where she carelessly tossed her dress onto a chair and struggled into her PJs. Brushing her teeth, she was suddenly awash with excited expectation at the thought of being with Nick the following evening. As she turned out the light and crawled between the sheets, the last thought she had was Nick's unspoken promise.

THERESA TOLD NICK she wanted to see Nicole before they left and tell her goodbye. About an hour later, they returned to the villa. Nick had set out all the leftovers for lunch and by the time they ate and were loaded and ready to go it was after four. As soon as they had disappeared down the driveway Nick was on the phone to Jas.

"Get over here, woman! I can't stand another moment without you."

Jas replied, "Okay, on my way." She hung up and just stared at the phone in disbelief. *If only he really meant that.*

Jas and Nick spent the day reliving the birthday party and reveling in each other's company. They had dinner, watched television and made love. *Maybe he did mean it. The one thing I do know is my love for Nick is real but... MOTHER, stop it!*

DAN THE WEATHERMAN became everyone's hero when Christmas morning dawned with a blanket of pure white snow turning the city into an enchanted fairyland. When she left for seven-thirty mass on Christmas Day, she found that the snow made driving difficult, if not hazardous. She said a silent prayer of thanks when she arrived at the church without incident.

In spite of the weather, the church was packed to capacity and, as expected, the Christmas decorations were breathtaking. Two large evergreens stood sentinel on either side of the altar and were generously adorned with small white lights. Red poinsettias surrounded the base of the trees and also graced the entire breadth of the altar. A beautiful nativity display of porcelain figures was situated in the center of the dias. The mass was inspirational and insightful and Jas was once again haunted by that old Catholic guilt.

BECAUSE NICK WAS spending Christmas day with Nicole and her family, Jas accepted an invitation to have Christmas dinner in Aztec with her long-time friends, Yvonne and Allen Sullivan. They would be joined by Allen's parents, Gary and Shirley, who were visiting from Phoenix. After mass Jas went home and changed into more casual attire. Jas gathered up her gifts for Yvonne and Allen and drove to Aztec without incident. The sun was bright and warm and the snow was rapidly melting making the highway more travel friendly.

When Jas arrived, Allen ushered her in and gathered her into an embrace.

"Good gosh! How long has it been?" he asked pushing her back and looking her over.

"Probably since last Christmas, you old goat. You haven't changed a bit."

"You neither. How do you manage to stay so young?"

"Why, thank you. I'm flattered but how long's it been since you've had your eyes examined?"

"Humph! Just because I'm on a diet doesn't mean I can't look at the menu. Nothing wrong with my eyes. It's the rest of the body that's gone to hell." Allan's laugh dissolved into a cough.

Just then Yvonne entered the foyer. "Jas, it's about time you came to see us! We've missed your visits." Yvonne gave Jas a sisterly hug. "Gary and Shirley are anxious to see you, too. Allen, take her coat…"

"Yes, ma'am!"

Jas handed Yvonne the gift wrapped packages and then slipped her arms out of the coat sleeves with Allen's help.

"Jas! I thought we decided not to exchange gifts." Yvonne scolded.

"We did." Jas paused a brief moment before adding, "I changed my mind. Anyway, your wonderful dinner is gift enough. I can hardly wait for the stuffing."

"Come on in," Yvonne said and led Jas into the living room. The scent of burning cedar wood from the fireplace comingled with the aroma coming from the kitchen made the atmosphere warm and inviting.

Gary and Shirley were seated in the living room. Gary rose as Jas entered. "It is wonderful to see you, Jas. Shirley and I were trying to remember when we all last saw each other."

Jas took Gary's hand and then gave Shirley a hug. "I believe the last time we were together was the camping trip to Vallecito Lake several years ago."

"I think you're right..." Shirley said furrowing her brow. "Is that the summer Gary fell off the boat into the lake while fishing?"

"Now, now. Don't go bringing that up," Gary pleaded looking embarrassed.

Yvonne excused herself. She said, "I'll leave you four to insult each other while I finish dinner." Jas offered to help but Yvonne said, "You stay here and catch up with Gary and Shirley. Make it fast, dinner is in ten minutes."

AFTER DINNER AND clean-up, Jas begged off using icy roads as a reason for not staying later. When she arrived home, she changed clothes again preparing for a prearranged rendezvous with Nick. She slipped into something less casual and tastefully sexy. She hurriedly checked her makeup and, as she jammed her arms into her coat sleeves, she smiled thinking of the gift she had for Nick.

ON ONE OF their weekend excursions to Durango, Nick had seen a small *Russell* brass sculpture in an art store and commented on how much he liked it. Jas, wrestling with what to get Nick for Christmas, remembered the *Russell* they had seen last summer. She immediately contacted the store and inquired about the sculpture.

The clerk said, "Yes. I know that piece well, unfortunately we sold it."

Jas' heart sank. *Dammit. It was perfect.* She then asked, "How can I get one?"

The clerk chirped, "We'll be happy to order one for you."

Jas breathed a sigh of relief. She so wanted this for Nick. "That's wonderful. Can I have it shipped directly to me here in Farmington.

"Yes, of course."

"How long will it take to get here?" Jas asked.

"Usually, not more than a week."

That's plenty of time before Christmas. "Okay, go ahead and order it."

"Certainly. Which credit card will you be using?"

"Oh," Jas was so happy to get the piece she had forgotten to ask the price. "How much is it?" When she was told the price she was glad she was sitting down.

"It's a steal at $500.00."

Jas gulped. Her mind raced. She didn't want to spend that much but, after all, it was perfect. She gave her credit card number and mailing instructions and never looked back. She was satisfied and didn't regret the purchase for an instant. It would look beautiful in Nick's library. She could hardly wait for Christmas to give it to him.

WHEN JAS ARRIVED at Nick's villa, he greeted her at the door with a quick kiss on the cheek.

"Here, let me take your coat," he offered. "How was your dinner with your friends?"

Jas, trying not to drop the gift, answered as she struggled with getting her arms out of the sleeves. "Just great. It was wonderful to see them."

"Christmas with the kids was delightful. You wouldn't believe the stuff those little monsters got..."

Jas then handed the gift to Nick. He exclaimed "Wow! What in the world is this? I already have a set of weights."

"It's your Christmas slash birthday gift." Nick just stood there holding the package. Jas had waited long enough so she demanded, "Go ahead and open it! After all, Christmas is almost over."

"Well, when you put it that way..." Nick then, very methodically and painstakingly, unwrapped the sculpture. He sucked in his breath when he saw the *Russel* and exclaimed, "I don't believe it! How in the world... This is so totally unexpected."

He leaned over and gave Jas a kiss on the cheek before moving into the living room and reverently placing the piece on the fireplace mantle. Jas thought she detected a tear in Nick's eyes as he ran his fingers over the brass cowboys.

Nick turned to Jas and said, "I'm overwhelmed. Thank you so much." Then as an afterthought, he added, "I know this sounds pedestrian, darling, but you shouldn't have."

Jas was elated that Nick was so taken by her gift. She replied, "I knew how much you liked it and besides, what do you get the man who has everything and I do mean *everything*."

He knew exactly at what she was hinting. He put his arm around her waist and they stood for a few moments admiring the *Russell* together.

"Oh, my gosh," Nick said. "With all this excitement, I almost forgot. I have something for you."

He went to the tree and retrieved a small gift wrapped package nestled among the branches and handed it to Jas. She tentatively took the gift. She was almost afraid to open it not wanting to be disappointed as she was hoping for something committal, like a ring maybe.

"Well, go on," Nick said impatiently. "Open it."

Jas managed a weak smile and finally mustered up the courage to unwrap the box. Inside was a beautiful gold cross pendant suspended on a gold chain.

"Oh, Nick. How utterly perfect," she exclaimed, "I really love it." And she did really love it. It wasn't the coveted ring but, nevertheless, it was very special.

Nick, looking pleased with himself for having selected the perfect gift took it from her and said, "Here, let's try it on," and gently extracted the cross from the velvet cushion. "I'm so glad you like it."

"Like it, I love it!" Jas put her hand to her throat touching the cross as Nick fumbled with the tiny C-ring clasp.

"I agonized over what to get you and decided with your religious devotion and all, a cross would be appropriate," Nick said as he finally managed to fasten the chain. Before he stepped back, he kissed her on the back of the neck.

I will never take this off no matter what. This will be a permanent appendage never to be removed. Jas, lost in her musings, was snapped back to the present when Nick announced, "And, drum roll maestro, if you please!" He turned his back for a minute and bent to retrieve something from under the tree. When he straightened he had in his outstretched hands the *Story Teller* Kachina. It was adorned with red and green ribbon. He handed it Jas.

Now it was Jas' turn to suck in her breath. "Oh, my God, you don't mean it. Is it really for me?"

"Absolutely, after all, what do you get the woman who has everything, and I do mean *everything*."

Does he mean that or is he just being nice?

Then Nick said, "You know, my dear, you love it much more than I ever could and I want you to have it. I hope it brings you as much joy and pleasure as you've brought me."

The rest of the night was indeed filled with joy and pleasure — for both!

...and so it began....

PART TWO
...AND SO IT CONTINUES...

6
GATHERING CLOUDS

As the work on the mansion continued, it had gone from simple redecorating to significant remodeling. Jas spent most of her spare time with Nick, and as winter dissolved into spring, the relationship remained unchanged. Not that it was bad, it's just that Jas was head-over-heels in love with Nick and she hoped with all her heart to be a permanent part of his life. In that way, she was still an old fashioned girl. Nick had never said anything that led her to believe there would be a future together, nor did he say anything to the contrary.

That old phantom planted by her mother haunted her with a vengeance. Its power over her was growing, always skulking behind her thoughts. Now when Nick joked about other women, Jas became anxious about the relationship. The encounters he described were benign, that is, if one could believe what he said. Jas, however, was beginning to question whether his intentions were to make her jealous or whether there was some other ulterior motive behind all of it.

Is he just using me? Am I so blind that I can't see it? Is this going to end just as mother predicted? Nick will be gone and I'll be nothing more than a vague memory – if even that.

A ripple of panic caused her to tremble.

What are my choices? If I give him up, my life will be in sham-
bles. Even though Nick has never said the words "I love you" his
actions seem to indicate he does. Okay then, if he continues to show
love, I'll be patient. Well, at least for the time being or until the
remodel is complete. If nothing changes, I'll have to make that awful
decision. For now, I'll continue to love him and show that love just as
before with the determined expectation that he will eventually recip-
rocate. Patience is not my long suit so I'll just pray that the wait
would be brief and in the end fruitful.

Because of the intense emotions Jas experienced having
been with Nick, both good and bad, she knew she would never be the same without him. With every doubt and every question the phantom created by her mother became stronger.

What Jas didn't know was that Nick had been pressured,
or more aptly forced, to marry Stephanie. It was a day from
hell when Nick received the letter from Stephanie informing
him she was pregnant. He had been home on leave from the
Air Force only a few days but long enough to have impregnat-
ed her. Even though he cared for Stephanie, he never really
was in love with her. Nonetheless, he would tell her he loved
her when they married and thereafter and more frequently
after their daughters were born. When Stephanie died, Nick
made a vow to himself that he would never profess his love
again unless he meant it. Even if he meant it, he wouldn't say
it unless he was absolutely sure.

ONE EVENING, AFTER completing a small painting job,
Jas noticed Nick was not himself.

"Nick? Honey, are you feeling okay?" she asked concern
in her voice.

"What? Oh, yeah. Maybe I have a touch of the flu."

"You don't look too good."

Nick responded, "I've been extremely tired for some reason. Maybe it's because I've been vomiting. I've also had stomach cramps and diarrhea most of the day."

"I think we should go to the ER…"

"Nonsense! The symptoms are exactly like the flu and, as you know, there is nothing they can do for that," Nick said.

The irritation in his voice bled through so Jas decided to back off and just keep an eye on him. "Why don't you go lay down? I'll clean up the brushes."

"Thanks, honey. Think I will."

Jas completed the clean up and went into the bedroom where she observed Nick. He was pale and his breathing was shallow. On the verge of panic, she determined he was indeed ill and needed medical attention.

"We need to get you to the hospital," Jas urged.

"No! I'll be all right. Just let me rest."

Jas sat nearby closely watching. When she realized he was fading, and after much coaxing, she finally got him into her car and raced him to the emergency room at Sacred Heart Hospital.

Nick was admitted and diagnosed with a severe case of listeria.

Jas sat in the waiting room wringing her hands and praying. She jumped up when she saw a nurse coming her direction.

"Ms. O'Connor, Mr. McGregor is stabilized."

Jas crossed herself, "Thank God."

"You did the right thing bringing him in. He would not have lasted the night without medical attention."

Jas stood silent just nodding her head. She was too emotional to speak.

The nurse continued, "There have been over two hundred deaths and thousands sickened nationwide as a result of this current outbreak. Do have any idea where he could have contacted the bacteria?"

Jas crossed her arms and rubbed them with her hands. "I don't know…" then she remembered. "He had lunch at his favorite deli, *The Radish*. He loves the salad bar. We usually eat lunch together but today I couldn't go."

"You're lucky. From what you say, my guess is that's where he contacted it. A salad bar is an ideal incubator for the bacteria. I'll let the Health Department know and ask them to conduct an immediate investigation."

"Thank you for the update," Jas said and again took up her vigilance in the waiting room.

Nick had dehydrated and was running a high fever. For the next two days he remained in a semiconscious critical condition. Jas spent as much time by his side as her job and the hospital personnel would allow.

The day nurse wasn't as considerate as the night staff and "Nurse Ratchet" ran a tight ship enforcing visiting hours with an iron fist. On the third day when Jas arrived, Nick was sitting up enjoying lunch which consisted of warm clear broth and Jello. Jas was so excited to see how much improved he was she couldn't control her exuberance.

She rushed to his bedside. "Nick! Look, you're eating. I was so frightened, I…I…" Then she could no longer control her emotions and the days of pent up fear and apprehensions, she exclaimed, "Damn you anyway! How dare you scare me like that!"

Nick smiled and croaked, "Right. This was all contrived to upset you and test your love. I see it worked."

Jas slumped and sat down on the side of the bed. "Guess that was pretty childish. I thought I'd lost you. I was worried sick. It's certainly good to see how much you've improved." She kissed his cheek and then slid her hand under the sheet and slowly moved it down his torso caressing him as she did. She leaned over and whispered in his ear, "As soon as you recover I'm going to ravage your body, take you places you've never been and you're going to love every second of it."

"H-m-m-m, anticipation is part of the experience. I'm already lovin' it." was Nick's weak reply.

At that moment, the door burst opened and Nurse Ratchet briskly walked in. She could have been an actress as she never missed a cue. Jas quickly removed her hand from under the sheet but not before Ratchet surmised what was going on.

"Visiting hours are *over*. You have to leave NOW."

"Okay, okay, I'm going." Jas squeezed Nick's hand and started toward the door. Nick whispered her name and she turned just as *he* blew *her* a kiss. She responded by throwing him her signature departure kiss.

Once in the corridor Jas slumped against the tile hospital wall. Her knees turned to jelly as she slid down the wall into a sitting position on the floor. She wrapped her arms around her legs, buried her head in her knees and quietly sobbed tears of relief and gave thanks to God for Nick's improved condition. He had turned the corner. She could not bear to think of a life without Nick.

Nick continued to improve and was released from the hospital a day later upon a promise that he would have a caretaker at home to help him.

Nick, looking at Jas, asked, "Is there any way you could…"

Jas didn't hesitate a second, "Of course! I wouldn't have it any other way."

"Nor would I."

Wonder what that means? Am I the one he wants to be with or am I just convenient?

Basically Nick was very healthy and once home he gradually regained his strength thanks to Jas' undivided attention. She closed her business for a week in order to be with him. She ensured he took his meds timely and prepared healthy meals and encouraged him to eat and drink as much as he could. Nick's medications made him drowsy so he slept quite a bit cradled and snug in the knowledge he had a guardian angel watching over him—an angel that he deeply loved.

BECAUSE OF NICK'S extensive experience in aviation and airport administration he was recruited by the FTA to become a board member on the Airport Commission. Nick was honored to participate and had been on the board for two consecutive terms. It wasn't a huge commitment as they met once every other month unless there was a special project.

"With plans for a new airport expansion underway," Nick told Jas, "I will have to devote more time reviewing the construction from an aviator's point of view."

"Certainly. That's an important part of the new structure. Future aviators will thank you for your part in making the airport pilot-friendly."

"Pilot-friendly? Did you just coin a new phrase?"

"Probably, but feel free to adopt it as your own if you like."

"I just may. I like the way it sounds. Thanks."

Thursday afternoon Jas was arranging some new accent pieces in her shop when the phone rang. She smiled when she heard Nick's voice.

"Hi Jas! Look, honey I'm sorry to have to do this, but the Airport Commission has called a special meeting tonight so I can't make it for dinner. Forgive me?"

"Of course, but you'll have to make it up *somehow*."

Nick laughed. "I'll see what I can do. Gotta run, but I'll call you later."

Jas replaced the phone feeling disappointed at the last minute change of plans. She remembered some of her girlfriends had been asking her to get together with them. She hardly saw them anymore so this would be a good opportunity for a girl's night out. With that in mind, Jas placed a call to Cheryl, one of her oldest and closest friends.

"Jas! What a surprise. Is everything all right?"

Jas laughed. "Yes, everything is just fine."

"That's a relief. I never hear from you anymore and I had a sudden premonition something terrible had happened."

"Guess I deserve that. I was wondering if perhaps some of the old gang could get together this evening for dinner and a movie. Do you think Connie and Marilyn would be up for it?"

"I certainly am and I will call Connie and Marilyn. I'm sure they can rearrange their evening since this is a *rare* occasion."

"Oh, stop! You're making me feel guilty."

"GOOD!" Cheryl paused momentarily then asked, "Where and when do you want to meet?"

"How about *All Seasons* at six? It's just up the street from the *Bijou* so we can walk to the theater after dinner."

"Perfect! That new Bond movie is playing and I've been dying to see it. Six it is, with or without Connie and Marilyn."

As it turned out, everyone was eager to see Jas. Dinner was fun, laced with lots of laughter as the foursome exchanged stories as they caught up on each other's lives.

Connie, looking very much like a conspiratorialist, asked, "Say Jas, are you seeing anyone? You've been so evasive, we were just wondering if a new romance is encompassing all of your time."

"Well, not really," Jas replied. *Nick has demonstrated he wants to keep our romance secret. After all, I certainly wouldn't want to embarrass him and I don't want to appear like a lovesick fool so I'm not going there.*

"Un-huh!" Cheryl said and Jas detected a hint of sarcasm in her voice.

Even though they have been lifelong friends, it's none of their business.

AFTER DINNER THE women walked to the *Bijou* and lined up on the sidewalk outside the ticket window. Jas stepped up to purchase her ticket when the sound of a familiar laugh caught her attention. She glanced over her shoulder as she crammed her change into her purse and the smile melted from her face. Across the street she saw Nick leaving an expensive restaurant with the woman from Carlton Realty. They appeared pretty chummy as they walked toward Carlton's car parked just a block away. Cheryl followed Jas's gaze and frowned.

"Say, Jas, isn't that McGregor over there? Wonder who he's with? My, my, his late wife was movie star beautiful. He certainly has slipped." She shook her head in disgust.

Jas felt a tight knot form in her gut. All of her doubts and pent up emotions made her tremble and she tried to hold back her tears. *I can't fall apart here in front of my friends. The gossip would never die down. How could Nick lie and betray me like that? Even worse, Carltons married. Guess she could cover by claiming she was entertaining a client if they were caught.*

Jas wanted to run away but that wouldn't be wise so she toughed it out.

After the movie, Marilyn suggested, "Come on, let's go over to *Sully's* and have a nightcap. It's just across the street and it's too early to call it a night."

"Oh, no thanks. I have an early morning so I should get on home," Jas lied as she started toward her car parked just up the block. She turned and added, "I enjoyed this so much and we must do it again soon." Her friends just stood and stared after her.

As Jas closed her car door and she could no longer hold back the tears. She slumped over the steering wheel and wept. A very conflicted Jas cried herself to sleep that night.

IT WAS COMMON knowledge that the Carltons had made a financial killing in the real estate market before the collapse. After the collapse they made another killing buying fore-closed properties and then reselling them, oftentimes offering their own financing. Looking back, Jas remembered seeing a Lexus bearing the Carlton Realty logo on its door panels exiting the Desert Rose Estates where Nick lived. This happened on more than one occasion. Jas would pass the Carlton vehicle at about the same location at about the same time several times a week. Did Nick have another contract or, was it something else?

Turbulence raged in Jas' mind and heart. She massaged her temples with her fingers in an attempt to quell the anger and confusion she was feeling. *Should I just cut my losses and boogie or should I hold out hope that he will eventually return my love? My mind is saying go but my heart is saying no. Heart wins every time! Shut up, Mother! I'll make my own decisions. I'm not ready to throw in the towel just yet.*

IT WAS MID-SUMMER and the San Juan County Board of Commissioners staged their annual Law Enforcement Appreciation Banquet to honor law enforcement personnel with five, ten, fifteen, twenty and twenty-five years of service or more. This was an elaborate formal dinner dance and all of law enforcement received invitations as well as the local merchants who supported LE during the year. Jas had attended the affair in the past with casual friends; she liked dressing up and going out. Jas was hopeful that Nick would agree to take her. He was sprawled on the sofa reading the newspaper when Jas entered the room. *What've I got to lose?*

"Nick," she began, "the law enforcement banquet is Saturday."

"Un-huh," Nick uttered, only halfway paying attention to her.

"It's a formal affair and I've always loved going. Would you take me?"

"Sure, why not."

Jas blinked in disbelief. She expected him to decline knowing how much he disliked those kinds of things but much to her surprise, he accepted. "YOU WILL?" she blurted.

"Yep. I'll dust off the ole tux and hope it still fits. It hasn't been out since…well, I can't remember since when. Probably one of the girls' weddings." Nick relished wearing his tuxedo knowing how handsome he looked, that is if he interpreted the glances from the opposite sex correctly–which he usually did.

WHEN THE DAY of the dinner dance arrived Nick called Jas at work, "Honey, something has come up that I must attend to. I won't be able to pick you up but I will meet you there. I don't anticipate being too late. Save me a seat."

Jas was disappointed but her voice never betrayed her. *Wonder what kind of emergency had come up this time demanding his immediate attention. Carlton? Where there's smoke, there's fire.* Once again, Jas was confused and tormented and the dark phantom rose in her mind.

THE LE EVENT always had a large turnout and the banquet hall was crowded when Jas arrived. She had selected a knee-length spaghetti strapped satin dress with a sweeping skirt of ivory chiffon and, despite her anguish, she looked lovely. She snaked through the tables and found some seats close to the bandstand. As soon as she sat down, an old friend Jas had dated several years before approached and sat down on the chair Jas was saving for Nick.

"Jas, how nice to see you."

"Oh, hello, Brandon. Nice to see you as well. How have you been?" As she chatted with Brandon, she kept watching the door for Nick. She finally spotted him and waved as he came in. Nick smiled and strode across the room and sat down on the other side of Brandon. Jas introduced them and they shook hands.

"I hope I'm not intruding," Brandon said.

"Of course not," Nick assured him. "You are more than welcome to join us if you'd like."

"That's very kind," Brandon said looking around. "But I'm here with a date and need to get back to my table or I will be in big trouble." He smiled as he got up.

"Jas, great to see you and it was a pleasure meeting you, Nick."

As Brandon left, Jas stared at Nick for a moment. *Was Nick trying to make it appear as though she wasn't his date?* She tried not to listen to the taunting voices and made light conversation as dinner was served.

Suddenly Nick whistled softly and spoke under his breath to no one in particular, "Hello Baby, where have you been all my life?" Jas put down her fork and followed Nick's gaze to the table opposite theirs and recognized Shelly Lyons looking absolutely ravishing in a red satin gown, her fabulous blond hair swept into a very becoming up doo. Jas then observed the back of Tom Lyons as he left his table heading toward the bar probably to get a drink for Shelly and himself. They obviously had just arrived. Tom and Shelly were condo-dwellers and shared the same complex as Jas so Jas knew them and was actually good friends with the couple. In fact, Shelly had become a confident of sorts. Shelly knew Jas was seeing someone but didn't know the details.

After all that had taken place during the evening and in the recent past with Nick, Jas had reached her limit. Nick's salacious comment regarding Shelly just reinforced his disrespect for her feelings. She knew the comment was meant for her benefit. Irked, Jas got up and walked over to Shelly's table. A very surprised Nick followed her every move with his eyes. Jas greeted Shelly and sat down in Tom's chair.

"Hi, Shelly."

"Well, just look at you. Jas, you're beautiful." Shelly gave her a warm hug.

Without looking toward Nick, Jas said, "My date," Jas jerked her head toward Nick, "wants to know where you've been all his life. I think he wants to meet you."

Shelly looked surprised. She knew that Jas knew she was married. Shelly raised her eyebrows in a questioning gesture to which Jas immediately replied, "He's my date or whatever sitting directly opposite you with his eyes bulging. I'm leaving since I'm not feeling well and thought you might want to introduce yourself to him. His name is Nick 'Rat-Bastard' McGregor."

Shelly immediately connected the dots and nodded comprehension. As Jas started to get up, Shelly took her arm and said, "Honey, you stay put. Someone is going to get his come-uppance. Tell Tom I'll be right back. You go ahead and drink my margarita if you like. I have a job to do."

Jas, not wanting to miss the come-uppance sat back down. Shelly rose, adjusted her gown, ran her hand up her neck smoothing the up doo. She took a deep breath, squeezed Jas' shoulder and sauntered toward Nick. Nick sat taking all of this in. He was transfixed. He didn't know what to think or expect.

Shelly approached Nick and whispered in his ear, "Nicky, would you dance with me?"

Nick was stunned but flattered. The couple walked onto the dance floor and Nick took Shelly in his arms in a close dance stance.

Shelly stated, "Oh, Nicky, I can hardly breathe, but that's okay because what I have to say is for your ears only."

Nick was unsure what to think and glanced in Jas' direction as if to ask "What do I do now?"

Shelly, whispered to him as they danced, "I trust you realize that your date is one of the most beautiful women I've ever known, both inside and out, and there you are scouring the room ogling other women."

Nick looked stunned. *My God, what have I done. Jas may never speak to me again.* Not knowing what else to do he kept dancing.

Shelly continued, "As for me, I know your kind. Need I say more? I think you've just burned your last bridge with Jas. In essence, you've thrown Aladdin's Lamp back into the ocean and you have no idea what you've lost."

With that Shelly pulled away from Nick and walked off the dance floor leaving him to deal with the embarrassment. However, before she got too far, she turned and said, "Oh, by the way, I hope you enjoy the rest of your evening. We're leaving."

Shelly went back to her table and the three of them, Shelly, Tom and Jas, left the banquet hall. Jas never looked back.

ONCE OUTSIDE, JAS asked in an anxious voice, "Shelly, tell me what happened." Before Shelly could speak, Jas' cellphone began to ring. She knew it was Nick and she ignored it.

Shelly reiterated the conversation. "I think somewhere along the way Nick had an epiphany. At least, the expression on his face changed reflecting one of enlightenment."

Jas' cellphone rang again and Shelly, looking at Jas, raised her eyebrows waiting to see what she would do. Jas ignored it again.

Shelly said, "Well, what's that they say, too little, too late. I think we've all had enough fun for one evening. Come on, let's go home."

Once Jas was home and alone she examined her feelings. She was unsure and was already rethinking her strategy. As she sat there pondering her future, something inside her reassured her that she had done the right thing and she suddenly felt peaceful. *It's about damn time. Now he knows how it feels.*

AFTER SHELLY WALKED off, Nick stood there for a moment trying to comprehend what had just happened as he watched Jas leave. He had come here for Jas and now she was furious at him. More than being embarrassed he was horrified that his teasing and clowning around may well have cost him the future with the woman he loved more than life itself. He hurried out to the parking lot and hit the speed dial on his cell with Jas's number. No response. He tried again and again with the same results. He finally gave up and went home.

NICK CALLED JAS the next day. Still no response. When he got no response the third day he decided to seek her out. He had had time to ponder his ill-advised actions and the disastrous consequences.

Nick timed his visit to arrive just as Jas got home from work. She was thus unable to avoid him.

I was insensitive and wrong. I need to make it up to her if it isn't too late. I never intended to hurt her. She's too sensitive and I'm too insensitive–what a dangerous combination.

When Jas drove up, Nick was standing outside his car leaning against the passenger door. She ignored him as she exited her vehicle and started toward her front door. Nick caught up to her, took her arm and gently turned her toward him.

Nick took her in his arms and said, "Jas, I am so sorry I hurt you. I didn't mean to. That's just something guys do, you know, look at pretty women. I realize now how insensitive I was. Give me a second chance and I promise I'll never hurt you again." Then after a short pause, he added, "Besides, I'm not up to tangling again with that Shelly woman."

That little comment broke the ice and they laughed and cried at the same time.

Jas hugged Nick and replied, "Okay, Nick, one more chance." And she made a silent promise to herself, *Only one more chance, then it's over forever.*

Once again things returned to normal, except, that is, for Nick's discernible attitude adjustment.

…and so it continued…

PART THREE
...AND SO IT ENDS...

7
SEVERE STORMS

Nick stood at the workbench stirring paint while Jas prepared the brushes. Watching Jas, he suddenly felt very insecure. *Has Jas' feelings for me changed? She never tells me she loves me anymore. Is she thinking of leaving me? God, I hope not! Life would be empty and I'd be lost without her.* As Nick studied Jas more closely, she glanced at him and smiled. *She still has love in her eyes and expresses love through her body language, but she quit saying so and I miss that.*

Work continued on the remodel and their personal situation improved but not all to Jas' liking. Nick threw her a few crumbs now-and-then but he still wouldn't say those three little words Jas so desperately wanted to hear. She knew Nick guarded his feelings carefully so she, too, reined in her desire to pour out the pent up reservoir of love she was feeling. She never again told him that she loved him. *Woman does not live on crumbs alone!*

JUNE IN FARMINGTON provided a prelude to the expected blistering hot summer. It did not disappoint. As the summer progressed, Jas continued to observe with regularity, although not every day, the silver Lexus with Carlton Realty logos on the door panels exiting the estates at the same time she was arriving. It struck her as being odd that they would encounter each other as often as they did and always at the same time and usually at the same place.

"Nick, I've noticed a Carlton Realty vehicle roaming around here quite often. It looks like it's coming from your place." Jas noticed Nick stiffen. *Hum. Wonder what that means.* "Do you know who it is?"

"No! Don't think I've seen it." Then after a pause, "What difference does it make anyway?"

More red flags. That was a blatant lie. Jas thought back to the evening she had seen Nick and Adell Carlton leaving the restaurant together confirming that Nick knew Carlton. Why would he lie about it unless he had something to hide?

AS JULY LOOMED hot and dry, the desert continued to wilt from the excessive heat. Even the most resilient foliage was beginning to dry up. Jas had to marvel, however, at the tenacity of the cacti and its stubborn insistence on surviving in such a hostile environment. One could look in any direction and see the heat waves rise. Even the lizards were seeking cover. Jas was grateful she had access to a private swimming pool and took advantage of it at every opportunity. Her suntan was coming along nicely but Nick, having tanned the previous several summers, had instant tan in just a few weeks. His swarthy appearance only added to his good looks.

At the end of July, we'll have been together a year. I wonder if Nick even remembers. Don't think it means the same for him but I'm going to make it a memorable one anyway.

Jas decided not to mention to Nick the special dinner was to celebrate their anniversary and set about planning the celebration for the two of them. She purchased a bottle of champagne to commemorate the occasion and spent one whole afternoon shopping for a special outfit.

Saturday evening, July 24, Jas started dinner preparations. She wrapped potatoes in foil and put them in the oven to bake while she cut up a salad. She stood back and looked around as she wiped her hands on a kitchen towel. She decided dinner preparations were far enough along that she could change into her new dress.

Nick was on the patio fussing with the grill and the glass wind chime tinkled in the summer breeze as Jas approached wearing her new dress.

"WOW!" he exclaimed. Nick seemed genuinely at a loss for words as he looked her over. He finally managed to say "Where did you come from and what did you do with Jas?"

Jas twirled to give him the full view of the halter top back and looked over her bare shoulder in a coquettish-way batting her long eyelashes and smiled a sweet smile that held a forbidden promise.

"Let's forget dinner and get straight to the main event," he purred.

"Not a bit of it," Jas protested, feigning anger. "I've slaved over a hot stove for at least five minutes and we're going to indulge in my efforts."

"Yes ma-am! Your wish is my command."

The evening was glorious and the dinner never more delicious. Jas was happy in an apprehensive sort of way. She experienced new feelings coming from Nick that she couldn't identify or explain as nothing monumental had really happened and neither of them had mentioned their anniversary. It was just his mannerism or something she couldn't quite describe. She caught him looking at her with different eyes, However, her anxiety was still holding her captive.

I wonder what's going on in his head. Is it the wine or is something really happening? Probably wishful thinking.

After dinner, they sat on the patio swing and held hands in silent appreciation of the cool evening. Jas finally said it was time to clean up and Nick went with her into the kitchen. Jas was at the kitchen sink preparing to put the dishes into the dishwasher when Nick walked up behind her. He took her wet hand in his and said, "You know how much I value and respect your opinion. I want you to be the first to know I've fallen deeply in love with someone very special and I intend to ask her to marry me."

Jas jerked her hand away from Nick. *What!*

Nick paused for a brief moment but apparently didn't detect Jas' reaction. He then continued, "I know now she's all I've ever wanted. She's beautiful, intelligent, a joy to be with and I feel she loves me as much as I love her. I'd be a fool to let her slip through my fingers. I have a ring and I'd like your take on it before I give it to her. I want everything to be perfect."

Nick then slipped his hand into his shirt pocket to retrieve the ring.

Jas just stared at Nick in wild-eyed disbelief. Her face contorted into something almost unrecognizable. Nick looked at her expression and drew back in shock. *What had gone wrong?* Suddenly the reality of the moment hit him like a fist to the gut. *After all we have been through together and all we have shared…I was certain she would see through my ruse. Certainly she knows this is meant for her–that she is the woman with whom I want to share my life.*

As thoughts tumbled through his mind, Jas whirled away from him and planted both hands on the edge of the counter as though she was about to topple over. Suddenly everything seemed to move in slow motion. Her head fell back as an anguished cry ripped the air. Deep, pitiful sobs made her shoulders quake. *Mother had been right all along. Never trust a man.* Her limbs trembled and anguish roiled in the pit of her stomach. "NICK!" she screamed. "I love you!"

"Jas, honey… Let me explain." *Oh, God. What have I done?*

His voice sounded like a distant echo–some tiny indistinguishable din in the back of her mind. *The man I love wants another. Why couldn't it have been me? Why hadn't he told me there was someone else in the picture? WHY? WHY? WHY?* Her stomach clenched into a tight knot; her breath came in short and irregular gasps as her face reflected the fiery explosion within. In a moment of uncontrolled grief and rage, her hand snatched up a steak knife on the counter and she swung around facing Nick.

"Why-y-y-y…?" Her anguished scream shattered the air again.

Nick could only stare, his mouth open. *How could I have been such a fool?* Suddenly a sick realization washed over him and he rushed toward to her, his arms reaching out for Jas — his precious Jas.

In that moment their fate was sealed. The knife was suddenly engorged in his torso, buried nearly to the handle. Nick gasped in shock and fell to his knees clutching his chest, his shirt rapidly turning crimson. He looked at her with a strange expression, his lips fighting to form words. He slowly fell forward pushing the knife deeper into his chest. As he hit the floor, the ring rolled from his hand. Jas stared at it for a moment, then she gingerly plucked it from the floor. Twisting the ring in her fingers, she noticed an inscription on the inside: "*Jas,* Luv U *4-Ever, Nick.*"

Another cry erupted from the depth of her being. She crouched beside Nick, praying and hoping there would be another chance. *He loved me! Why did he never tell me…?* Everything became surreal. In her confusion she unconsciously slipped the ring onto her finger. She looked down at Nick, blood seeping from the wound and forming a widening pool on the floor where he lay.

Have I killed the only man I ever loved? Oh, God. What am I to do?

Jas frantically grabbed the phone and dialed 911 hoping against hope she was not too late to save him.

"911…"

"Please, please hurry. A man has been stabbed. HURRY!"

"What's your address?"

Jas had dropped the phone and didn't hear the question. She knelt down beside Nick cradling him in her arms and praying. "Please God, please don't let him die. Please don't let him die. Nick, I love you. I love you…"

The 911 operator retrieved the address from the reverse directory and dispatched the EMTs and a squad car. The sirens grew closer as the emergency vehicles screamed up the driveway. Jas stayed where she was as the EMTs converged on the house.

Jas heard their gear clatter as they approached the patio. She called out, "In here, in the kitchen. Please, please hurry."

The EMTs followed her voice to the kitchen where she crouched still holding Nick. Gently taking her by the shoulders, one medic maneuvered her out of the way and began examining Nick.

"I'm afraid we're too late," he said as he searched for a pulse.

A painful groan escaped Jas' lips and she sagged against the kitchen counter.

The other medic, who had attached an intravenous tube to Nick's arm responded, "I'm afraid you're right. He has lost a lot of blood." He stood and jockeyed a gurney in position next to Nick's body, "Come on, let's get rolling."

The two EMTs gently placed Nick on the gurney and wheeled him out to the ambulance.

Oh, God, please, please, please…. Jas stood by watching in hopeful silence. *It seems like my whole life I've managed to destroy the good things that come my way. I didn't mean for this to happen! Will God ever forgive me?*

The police arrived just as the EMTs wheeled Nick out and immediately segregated Jas in another room. They began what some would refer to as an interview and others as an interrogation. Jas worked for attorneys the summer after she graduated college. She knew not to make any statements or answer any questions until she consulted an attorney so she invoked her constitutional right to remain silent and, upon doing so, was not questioned further. She knew this would add to the air of suspicion already surrounding her but she had no recourse. Her first inclination was to confess but having time to reconsider as the EMTs worked over Nick, she reasoned her confession would not bring Nick back and she was not into self-sacrifice that would serve no purpose.

Did I stab Nick or was it an accident when he rushed for me and pulled me into him? I can't remember, it happened so fast...I wouldn't have, couldn't have killed him. Oh God! I need time to think.

JAS WAS TAKEN to the police station and placed in an interrogation room. Because she exercised her right to confer with a lawyer, the detectives ceased questioning her further and allowed her the obligatory one phone call. During that summer working for attorneys, Jas became intrigued with criminal law and continued to follow interesting cases closely. Because of this, she knew who the best criminal lawyer was so she contacted him.

When Samuel "Salty" Morton arrived at the police station he was given access to Jas in the interrogation room. Putting his finger to his lips, he scribbled on a yellow legal pad cautioning her not to speak, that the room was wired and anything that was said was probably being recorded. Salty then began to write a series of questions to which Jas responded also in writing:

> Q. Have you made any kind of statement to authorities whether EMTs or law enforcement?
>
> A. No. I immediately asked for an attorney. They told me I wasn't under arrest at that time and they were just trying to piece together the details of what happened. I did not make a

statement; I gave no explanations or any other information to anyone. Did he... did he die?

Q. Yes, he died at the scene. He didn't make it to the hospital.

Jas collapsed into uncontrollable sobbing upon hearing that Nick actually died. Salty placed his hand on Jas' shoulder and patiently waited for her to regain control of her emotions. While Salty was waiting for access to Jas' interrogation room, the detectives had told him that Jas would be detained at the request of the DA at least until the initial investigation was concluded. He wrote:

Q. It appears you have become a suspect so you'll be processed into the jail tonight. How are you involved?

Thinking quickly knowing suspicion would be elevated if anyone suspected a relationship between her and Nick, Jas answered:

A. He commissioned me to remodel his home. I own an interior design shop downtown. He graciously suggested we do his remodel eve-nings and weekends leaving me free to run my one-man shop during business hours. I was to meet him at his home around six or six-thirty to show him some swatches and paint samples. I found him like that, tried to revive him and immediately called 911 for help.

Q. What did you say when you called 911?

A. Not sure. I think I said a man had been stabbed and needed medical assistance.

Q. When you arrived, did you notice anything unusual?

A. Not really unusual. It looked like someone was cleaning up after dinner. There were dirty dishes in the sink and the dishwasher was open. I was in such a state that there could have been an elephant in the kitchen and I wouldn't have noticed it.

Salty said, "That's enough for now. I'm going to check on advisement and bond. You can be held for 72 hours without being charged. Since it's the weekend, you will not have your first appearance in court until Monday. Everything depends on what the DA decides to do. Don't hold out any hope of getting a bond under a million dollars as that's the going rate on a murder one charge. Do you want me to contact anyone before this hits the papers?"

"My God, a million dollars! I couldn't even come up with ten thousand. Yes, please contact my close friend, Yvonne Sullivan. She lives in Aztec." Jas scribbled Yvonne's phone number on Salty's legal pad. "Let her know what happened and tell her I'm all right–for now anyway. Would you keep her apprised of the developments since I probably won't have access to the outside world for a while?"

Salty checked the phone number and said to Jas, "Yes, I'll keep in touch with Yvonne." You'll be processed into jail tonight. Tomorrow morning I will come see you first thing. In the meantime, just maintain your silence and composure. Are you okay?"

"Am I okay? No, I'm not okay." And with that she began to sob again.

Salty, regretting asking such an ill-advised question and feeling helpless, placed his legal pad in his brief case and left promising again to return the next day. The matron ushered a handcuffed Jas to a waiting jail transport vehicle that resembled an animal control cage on wheels.

JAS WAS TRANSPORTED to the San Juan County Jail and given an orange jumpsuit and a pair of rubber sandals, the usual jail garb. Her personal effects were confiscated and placed in a manila envelope with her identifying information written on it. It was then she remembered she had slipped the ring on her finger and was terrified that someone would notice the inscription.

The evidence custodian busied himself with recording the items taken from Jas. She toyed with the gold cross Nick had given her for Christmas; she had never removed it from the time he placed it around her neck. She hesitated taking it off and asked, "Would it be all right to keep my cross?"

"No! That's against regulations. Please hand it over," the custodian said in an authoritative voice.

Jas reluctantly gave it up but kissed it before she parted with it.

There seemed to be a lot of confusion in the booking area since it was Saturday night and a more-than-normal number of arrestees were being processed. Jail personnel was stretched to the limit and arrestees were being fingerprinted and booked as fast as possible. Jas was thankful that no one took time to really look at her personal belongings, especially the inscribed ring. They were entered in the log as one Seiko ladies watch, a gold/diamond ring, a pair of gold earrings and a gold cross pendant.

After she was fingerprinted and photographed she was provided a blanket and some toiletries and led to a cold sterile cell where she was locked up, sequestered from the rest of the jail population.

JAS SAT ON her bunk and buried her head in her hands. She couldn't control her sobbing. She had difficulty catching her breath and vomited into the stainless steel toilet bowl. Exhausted, she collapsed on the cold hard cot and fell into a fitful sleep fraught with dreadful dreams and a deep pain within.

When she was awakened in the morning by the jailers, she couldn't immediately remember where she was or what had happened. Then it all came back like a freight train rolling over the top of her. She was taken from her cell to the shower area. When she was alone, she turned on the shower and began washing off what remained of Nick's dried blood. Sobbing, she sank to her knees on the cement shower floor and tried to grab the blood-stained water spiraling down the drain.

What have I done? What have I done?

JAS WAS NOT allowed to mingle with the other inmates. Her breakfast was brought to her cell. Even if she had felt like eating, the bill-o-fare would have turned her off: gummy oatmeal, cold coffee and burnt toast. Everything was served on cheap plastic trays with cheap plastic utensils designed to prevent suicides she surmised. She immediately had the urge to vomit again and pushed the tray as far from her as she could.

She curled up on the hard cot and covered her eyes with her arm trying to remember the string of events that culminated in her being there. She didn't want to think of it as murder. To her, murder was the willful planning and taking of somebody's life. She didn't want Nick out of her life. Just the opposite, she wanted to spend her life with him. When she thought he was pushing her away and marrying someone else she couldn't cope with it. That's when she lost control of her senses and picked up the knife. *I don't kill him. Oh, God, how could I have done that? I don't understand. I loved him and still love him with my whole being. This has got to be a nightmare. If only I could awaken and have things the way they were before he died. If only he hadn't been such a bastard and tormented me so much with other women. If only I had had more trust in him. If only he would have expressed his true feelings for me and not*

*have left me to my own devices. If only, if only, if only... She was up
vomiting again.*

LATER THAT MORNING, Salty was escorted into Jas' cell
by a gum chewing jailer. His shirttail hung loose, his shoes
were muddy and his arrogant swagger indicated that he really
didn't give a damn.

"You may want to lose the gum, chum. And it wouldn't
hurt you to clean yourself up," Salty said with a look of disgust
on his face.

"Yeah. You're not my boss..."

"Yes. But I know your boss." Salty looked at the jailer's
nametag. "Want me to talk to him, Sandoval, badge number 18563?"

The jailer just shrugged, opened the cell and left.

Salty watched the jailer walk away, tucking his shirttail in
as he did so. Salty then entered the cell and looked at Jas with
apprising eyes, "How are you fairing?"

His question triggered more uncontrollable sobbing.
Guess that answers my question. Salty leaned against the bars
waiting patiently until she regained her composure. When
she calmed down, he sat down beside her on her bunk and
began to ask questions but only after cautioning her that the
cell also had ears.

"Jasmine, tell me what happened."

Jas sat twisting a tissue. She finally said, "I don't know
what happened before I got there, Mr. Morton, I found him
like that."

Salty sat down on the cot beside her; he had been taking
notes as they spoke."Mr. Morton is my father. Please call me
Salty or Sam."

"Okay," she replied weakly. Jas preferred using the name
Sam rather than Salty and did so from that day on.

"Did you say anything to the EMTs when they arrived?" his eyes never left hers.

"No."

"Did you say anything to the police? Anything at all?"

"No."

Salty rose and paced back and forth. "Explain to me exactly what happened from the time you left your house until you arrived at his house."

"Please, that pacing makes me nervous."

"Sure," Salty sat back down and positioned his legal pad on his lap.

Jas furrowed her brow, apparently trying to remember details. "Well, I left my house around 6:30 that evening. I always called him before I left to make sure he would be there when I arrived." Jas began to sob and dabbed at her eyes with the tattered tissue.

Salty had crossed his legs and leaned back against the cold cement block wall. "Take your time."

Jas sniffed once and then continued, "He answered and told me to come. I don't live far from him so it didn't take very long to get there." Jas' face darkened and her eyes grew cold when she said, "However, I did notice that same car with the Carlton Realty logos on the door panels coming out of the Desert Rose Estates. Remember, I previously told you about that. It happened quite often and I wouldn't be at all surprised if it came from Nick's place."

"Okay, you say you encountered 'that same car' often when you were going to his house. Can you describe the car?"

"I'm not very good when it comes to makes or models but I think it was a Lexus, silver with the Carlton Realty logos on the door panels."

"Can you describe the driver?" Salty asked, taking notes all the while.

Jas was showing signs of fatigue. She rubbed her crossed arms as she said, "She had dull blonde hair, straight and stringy. She appeared to be short and chubby from what I could tell just by looking through the windshield. Not a very attractive woman!"

"Did you travel the same route each time you went there?"

"Yes, there is only one main access road unless you want to take the long way around."

"Did you always go there at the same time of day?"

"No. It depended on when I got home from my shop." Jas paused, apparently thinking about her answer. "Sometimes I would stay late to meet with my clients who work a normal work day. This doesn't happen very often but I always try to accommodate potential customers. I need the business and the goodwill." After a moment, she continued, "I've concluded there was no rhyme or reason to the encounters with the car. It happened so often that it made me wonder, as I've said, if she was with him and left as soon as I called. That makes the most sense to me."

"Why would he care if you knew he was with someone? Were you romantically involved?"

Damn! Now what? "Well," Jas fumbled for an answer, "Well, don't you think it would be awkward at best to have me there while he was entertaining another woman since I needed his input regarding my suggestions on the changes he was making? Maybe she was married and he was having a covert affair with her. I don't know..."

"So, whatever the circumstances, he was obviously hiding something," Salty said. *Wonder if she thinks I'm buying her story? I sense she's not telling the complete truth and, the dead man must have been a complete idiot if he didn't see this intelligent, sensual woman for what she was and not have a romantic interest in her. Even in her disheveled state, she is captivating. I can't believe they weren't romantically involved and hence the reason she's been so evasive. Jealously would go to motive.*

"How did you usually proceed when you went to his place?" Salty finally asked.

"What do you mean?"

"Okay, you drove to his house, then what?"

"Oh, the door was always locked so I knocked. Since he was expecting me, he would unlock the door and let me in." Jas gulped, apparently in an attempt to stifle more tears.

"Sometimes during the day, when the light was best, he would have painted areas that we had agreed upon. If I had swatches or paint samples or accent pieces that I'd collected, we'd go over the placement of these items. We were never in a hurry to complete the work. He was deliberate and took his time making decisions. Remodeling can be expensive, especially if the clients keep changing their minds."

"Then what?"

"Then what, what?" Jas' voice was laced with irritation. "Then I would leave and go home. On the weekend our routine varied but during the week it almost never fluctuated."

"And this weekend...."

"This weekend we planned to work some around six or six-thirty Saturday evening." Thinking fast, Jas added, "I had plans later so I dressed for a late dinner before I left home."

"Was anyone else included in this 'late dinner'?"

Trapped! "I'd rather not say."

"It will probably become important."

Jas just remained silent and nervously bit her nails. Salty was growing skeptical by the minute and somewhat frustrated. After all, he was her lawyer and what she told him constituted privileged communication.

Salty stood. "Okay, at least for now."

Jas looked relieved. *I hope this interview is over.*

Jas looked disappointed when Salty continued, "Tell me exactly, and I mean exactly, what happened from the time you drove up to his house until you were brought to the police station."

Jas sighed. "I turned into the estates and, as I said before, I saw the Carlton Realty car leaving. I couldn't tell where it came from since we were on the main thoroughfare and not in any specific driveway."

"Did you mention the car to the police?"

"No, Like I said, I didn't make any statements."

"Okay, go on."

"I drove up to Nick's house and knocked on the door. When I knocked, the door gave a few inches. That was odd because, as I said before, he always kept the door locked. He lives in an upscale neighborhood and is conscious that he could be a target for a break in. I went in and called to him but he didn't answer. I thought then that possibly he had unlocked the door for me and that he was in the bathroom or otherwise indisposed. I called to him again but received no response. I went through the living room and as I walked past the kitchen I saw him lying there in a pool of blood." Jas, burying her face in her hands, completely broke down and wept.

Salty patted her on the shoulder and said, "Okay, take your time, I know this is difficult."

Jas swiped the tears from her cheeks and, in a shaky voice, said, "I ran to him and gently turned him over because he was lying face down. That's when I saw the knife sticking out of his chest. I was so distraught I didn't know what to do."

Jas, apparently trying to remember, rubbed her temples with her fingers before continuing. "I do recall thinking that if I got the knife out it would help so I tried to pull the knife out of his chest. I couldn't budge it. I was covered with Nick's blood from a large pool on the floor and from having cradled him in my arms. He was warm and I had hope that he was still alive. I even thought I detected some breathing.

I reached up and grabbed the phone off the counter and dialed 911. I stayed in that position until help arrived, talking to him, encouraging him to hang on. Everything is pretty much a blur from the time I saw him there and even now. How did all of this happen? How can I be a suspect? All I tried to do was help him."

Salty rubbed the back of his neck. He was still skeptical about her involvement. *I want to believe she's not the killer. At least this part of her story is convincing and coincides with the police reports. After all, what would her motive have been? She did have means and opportunity, but motive? It's possible they were involved in a romantic relationship and the green-eyed monster reared its ugly head. I see why Jasmine is the most likely suspect and why the authorities are trying to build a case against her. However, the Carlton Realty car is a lead worth pursuing. Maybe the driver thereof was the killer.*

8
TURBULENCE

Monday morning dawned bright and sunny. Jas' hearing was scheduled for 9:00 a.m. before the Honorable Clarence Ratkliffe, also known as the hanging judge by those who were destined to appear before him. The good thing about having a first appearance before Rats—his honor's nickname in the legal community–was that the case would, in all probability, be assigned to another judge for future hearings and trial. Rats was covering for the county court judges who were attending a judicial conference in Santa Fe. Today he was conducting first appearance advisements and assigning felony cases to district court judges. The likelihood of him assigning Jas' case to himself was little to none, especially since the case against Jas had not yet been officially filed by the prosecution.

Jas' first appearance before the court was the result of her having been incarcerated as a murder suspect over the weekend. Salty didn't have much hope of getting a bond set since the potential charge would be first degree murder. Upon learning that Rats would be conducting advisement hearings any glimmer of hope Salty might have had was quickly dissipating.

JAS APPEARED IN court as scheduled. She sat at the defense table beside Salty. He couldn't help but notice how haggard she had become. Her hair was carelessly pulled up in a ponytail, she was pale and listless and her red eyes were underscored with dark circles. The bright orange jail jumpsuit exaggerated her paleness. Salty was shocked at how much she had deteriorated since he saw her less than twenty-four hours before. He took her hand in an attempt to reassure her but she did not respond.

The judge read Jas her rights and asked if she understood them to which she responded with a weak "Yes."

Shuffling papers, the judge paused for a moment. Then he said, "The preliminary charge indicated on the warrant is first degree murder." He looked over his glasses at Jas.

"Your Honor!" Salty was on his feet.

"Yes, Mr. Morton," Rats removed his glasses and set them on his desk.

Salty cleared his throat, "Judge, my client, Ms. Zachary, has been a resident of San Juan County her whole life. She owns a business and…"

"Excuse me, Mr. Morton, if this argument is regarding bond, I'm obliged to stick to the bond schedule."

"I know but…"

"Bond is set at one million dollars, cash or surety." Then looking at Salty, he added, "You're welcome to take it up with Judge Ralston at your next hearing. I've assigned him this case." The judge banged his gavel, "Thelma, call the next case."

Salty breathed a sigh of relief because he knew Judge Wedge Ralston was a no-nonsense judge and was fair and reasonable.

Salty turned to Jas. "You'll be incarcerated until your next hearing," he said gathering up his paperwork and placing it in his valise. "We'll address bond again at that time."

Jas rose as a sheriff's deputy approached. "It won't do any good, Sam. I couldn't even make the ten percent on a hundred thousand. Thanks for trying anyway."

The deputy cuffed Jas and led her back to the holding area to await transportation back to the county jail.

AFTER THE HEARING, the first thing Salty did was file an Entry of Appearance with the court with a copy to the district attorney. Having filed said document, he was entitled to request all discovery which consisted of police reports and copies/descriptions of any and all physical evidence. The prosecution was bound by law to provide the defense with any materials, reports, photographs or other evidence that pertained to the case. Failure to do so would be a violation of the rules of criminal procedure and open the door for sanctions against the prosecution by the court.

When the entry was filed with the court and stamped with the date of filing, Salty went back to his office to begin the preparation for Jas' defense. This is what he was born to do. It was in his DNA and he approached the challenge with excited anticipation.

THE HEARING FOR the formal filing of charges was set for the next Wednesday before Judge Ralston at which time the prosecution was required to have the charges prepared.

Because of Jas' business and volunteer work, she had constant contact with most of the employees who worked in and for the judicial system. In order to avoid a conflict of interest or the appearance of impropriety, Chief Judge Chester Pritchett appointed the Bernalillo County District Attorney's Office in Albuquerque as special prosecutor. However, he ordered, all hearings and trial would be held in San Juan County and Judge Wedge Ralston would preside.

Judge Ralston was in agreement and did not see the need to recuse himself. He had had little or no personal contact with Jas. If the defense and/or prosecution did not object, he would remain on the case. As it turned out, neither side objected so it remained that the Honorable Wedge Ralston would preside over the case of *The People of the State of New Mexico v. Jasmine Zachary.*

MATTHEW JACOBY, ASSISTANT district attorney for San Juan County was present when Salty entered the courtroom the next Wednesday. Salty paused at the door and looked around. He approached Jacoby. "Hey, Matt, what happened? Thought we had a special pros?"

"Affirmative, however, too short notice for their man to be here so I'm covering formal filing," Jacoby answered.

Salty nodded. He then looked at Jas who was already seated at the defense table. Before he could speak to her, Jacoby handed him some paperwork.

"Here's a copy of the Information, Salty. Bernalillo faxed it over this morning."

Salty took the proffered document and sat down at the defense table. "How you doing this morning?" he asked Jas. Jas didn't answer. She just looked at him with sad eyes. *That's the second time I've asked that question. I must be an idiot.*

Salty then directed his attention to the document Jacoby had handed him and scanned it with a poker face. *Just as I anticipated. The prosecution filed the highest possible charge. Thank God there's no death penalty in New Mexico.*

After reading through the charging form which contained a list of proposed witnesses, he leaned closer to Jas and said as he turned pages of the charging document, "Jas, you're charged with first degree murder. This charge necessarily includes a charge of second degree murder. What that means is that the jury can choose between the two. They cannot find you guilty of both."

Jas registered no noticeable reaction. Salty looked at her with concern in his eyes. "Do you understand what I just told you?"

Jas nodded.

"Okay." Then after a slight pause, he asked, "Do you have any questions concerning what I have just told you?"

Salty looked at Jas expecting some response. She sat staring straight ahead. When he continued, his voice was laced with agitation. "The long and short of it is that you can be found guilty of first or second degree murder but not both or you could be found guilty of manslaughter which is also considered a lesser included charge. Do you understand?"

"Yes." Jas finally muttered as she hung and shook her head fumbling for a tissue.

Just then the door leading to the judge's chambers banged open and the court clerk stood and said in a loud voice, "ALL RISE!"

Judge Ralston entered and, with a sweep of his robe, took his seat behind the desk situated on a dias. Adjusting his glasses on his nose he looked out at the courtroom. His eyes came to rest on Jas just as the clerk announced her case.

"*People of the State of New Mexico versus Jasmine Zachary.*"

The judge then turned his attention to Salty and asked, "Is the defendant present?"

"Yes, Your Honor, she is." Salty stood and said, "I'm Samuel Morton, council for the defendant."

"Thank you, Mr. Morton but I think I know who you are." The judge looked down at the file on his desk. Then he asked, "Does your client wish to have the charges read aloud?"

"No, Sir, we do not."

The judge nodded his head.

"Your Honor, may I speak regarding bond."

"Go ahead." Judge Ralston said as he leaned forward tenting his fingers on his desk.

"Thank you, Your Honor," Salty turned and gestured toward Jas, "Ms. Zachary is a lifelong resident of San Juan County. She owns a business and property in Farmington." Salty put his hand on Jas' shoulder and continued, "She has no criminal history and it's not likely she would be a flight risk…"

"Mr. Morton, in the interest of saving judicial time," Judge Ralston said, cutting Salty off in midsentence, "I have reviewed the minute order of the initial advisement hearing and I'm aware of your argument to lower the bond. If this is where you're headed, let me be brief. It's the court's position that the charge is serious enough to warrant the million dollar bond." The judge then crossed his arms and leaned back in his leather chair. "I, therefore, decline to lower the bond."

"Thank you, Your Honor," Salty said and sat down. Jas was destined to stay in jail until at least the preliminary hearing.

JORDAN SLATER WAS Salty's "Della Street." She was an attractive feisty woman in her late forties. Her black hair was cropped short and styled in an easy doo. She couldn't be bothered with girlie things like make up and artificial nails and she wasn't concerned about being stylish. Slacks and flat heeled shoes were the order of the day.

Jordon had been employed as a paralegal, investigator and/or secretary in the judicial system for over twenty years. She was a computer whiz and Salty marveled at her tenacity, speed and skill. Jordan was competent and capable of performing all of the clerical duties associated with running the office. She was the quintessential "one-man show" and she was compensated handsomely for all the hats she wore.

Jordan's biker boyfriend, Dave Jennings, hung around the office when he wasn't working as a UPS driver. He was an ex-law enforcement officer and quasi-investigator.

Because of his uncanny resemblance to the oriental god Buddha, he was nicknamed *Buddha*. This was okay with him as it inferred deity. Buddha's law enforcement experience came in handy and Salty hired him on an *ad hoc* basis to investigate and interview witnesses.

Buddha relished working for Salty and didn't mind that he was asked to run the occasional errand. When he was required to make runs to the courthouse to file or pickup paperwork, he would almost always run into one of his past law enforcement confederates and avail himself of the opportunity to catch up on the latest gossip and determine which way the winds of public opinion blew. He was also friends with most of the judicial employees and enjoyed visiting with them when time allowed. He contended that it was not *what* he knew but *who* he knew that made him effective.

The law office of Samuel Morton, Esq. was hardly ostentatious and consisted primarily of a modest private office, small conference room dominated by an oversized oak rectangle table surrounded by six old-fashioned oak chairs and a reception area which sported floor to ceiling built-in bookcases along the back wall. The bookcases were crowded with neatly placed law books and legal periodicals. An oak half-circle antique counter separated Jordan's work space from the comfortable chairs in the waiting area. Salty had borrowed a closet adjacent to his office to store files and supplies.

Jordan was queen bee and ruled with an iron fist. Because the office was so small, she would not tolerate mess. Anything out of place upset the entire landscape, not to mention Jordon's disposition. When she spoke, they jumped. To say she was obsessive/compulsive was an understatement. Easier to pick up your mess than fight with a she-devil the men often joked. However, it was obvious that the three of them were quite the happy little family.

AS SOON AS he returned to the office, Salty said, "Buddha, run to the district attorney's office and obtain whatever discovery they have available on Jasmine Zachary. This early in the case I have little hope we would be provided with anything much more than the initial paperwork generated to hold Jas for arraignment but, who knows, there might be more. We need to know what we're up against as soon as possible."

"I'm on it!" Buddha said as he grabbed his helmet from the coat rack. Although he owned a Range Rover, when the weather permitted he chose to ride his Harley to the office. Salty insisted he park his hog in the rear of the building so as not to hinder or annoy his more sophisticated clients who looked at the biker community with distain.

The ride to the DA's office was short and the blaring horns and obscene insults didn't faze Buddha. He was able to snake his way through traffic and arrive at his destination in less than fifteen minutes.

Buddha waited patiently in the DA reception lounge for the paralegal assigned to the case to make him copies of the initial investigation report, arrest warrant and affidavit in support thereof.

"This is all we have at the present time, Buddha," Sheena said as she handed the copy to him. "We'll advise Salty when there is more available."

"Thanks, Sheena."

Buddha signed the receipt for the proffered document and returned to Salty's office. The affidavit was prepared by law enforcement and designed to convince a judge that the arrest was justified. The document gave a thumbnail description of the crime and was usually just barely enough to establish probable cause for the arrest. It stated Jas was found at the murder scene, covered with blood and cradling the deceased in her lap. It was a short scenario but was sufficient enough for a judge to sign.

"Well, I'm not surprised that this is it," Salty said and scratched at the stubble on his cheek. "It's still pretty early in the game but, it was worth a try. The only thing I see implicating our client is that she was at the crime scene."

Buddha sat quietly watching Salty peruse the scant warrant and affidavit in support, waiting in the event his boss had something more for him to do.

Finally Salty stood and slapped his desk with an open hand, "Jordon, prepare a request for a preliminary hearing. We'll make the prosecution reveal their theory. They'll have to in order to get the case bound over for trial." He sat back down and put his feet up on his desk, "I'll file it first thing tomorrow."

THE CRIME SCENE was still being processed so no forensic reports were yet available from that venue. The entire mansion was cordoned off with yellow crime scene tape. It was being dusted for fingerprints. Fibers and other evidence were being collected, marked and placed in plastic evidence bags. Telephone records and messages from the answering machines were examined and placed into evidence bags. DNA samples were taken from the still unwashed dishes in the kitchen and other sources such as combs and toothbrushes from the bathrooms.

It rained the day of the murder so photographs were taken of muddy tire tracks in the driveway. Salty stood outside the yellow crime scene tape and observed the process. He was allowed only limited access but he concluded that law enforcement was doing a respectable job processing the scene. Viewing the scene in person at this early stage would be an advantage later at trial. Besides, no good defense lawyer would go to trial without having viewed the scene.

MEANS, MOTIVE AND opportunity. Salty pondered the "big three" and wondered how Jas fit into the scheme in the eyes of the district attorney. Jas certainly had the means and opportunity, but how about motive? That was still a gnawing question. For now, all he could do was speculate. After all, his client was presumed innocent unless and until her guilt could be proven otherwise beyond a reasonable doubt.

9
WIND AND RAIN

The preliminary hearing was short and uneventful. The prosecution called only one witness to testify, Detective Sergeant Larry Bridges, the lead investigator. After Bridges was sworn in, Sylvia Cooper, the special prosecutor, began the questioning. Since preliminary hearings are, for the most part informal, Cooper remained at the prosecution table as she questioned Sgt. Bridges. She consulted her note pad for a moment before she began.

"Detective Bridges, please tell the court what you observed the day of the murder of Nicholas McGregor, the decedent in this case."

Bridges shifted in the confines of the witness chair and crossed his ankles, "Well, when we were contacted by 911, we were immediately dispatched to the scene. We arrived at the house just as the EMTs were loading the body into the ambulance."

"Okay. Go on," Cooper coaxed.

"The defendant," Bridges pointed to Jas, "was leaning on the kitchen counter and close to hysteria. She was covered with blood." Bridges paused and furrowed his forehead looking as though he was searching his memory. "At first, we didn't know if she was also a victim as she was covered with so much blood. When we determined she was the one that found the body, we isolated her in another room and questioned her." Bridges shifted in his chair.

"The EMTs said that the victim was still seeping blood and his body was warm." Then, reading from his notes, Bridges testified, "According to the medical examiner's report, the victim could not have lived more than two or three minutes after the wound was inflicted because of the great loss of blood and the victim was pronounced dead at the scene. The ME's report also stated that the defendant," Bridges point to Jas once again, "was the only suspect who could have perpetrated the murder since no other person was found or observed in close proximity to the scene. The time frame was too tight and Ms. Zachary herself discounted the likelihood of alternate suspects by stating she had not seen anyone at the scene when she first arrived."

Salty was on his feet, "I OBJECT!"

"On what grounds?" the judge asked with a quizzical look on his face.

"Hearsay statements. Your Honor, Sgt. Bridges is testifying to what he was told, not what he personally observed."

"Objection overruled. Mr. Morton, you know that the rules of evidence are relaxed at preliminary hearings." The judge then motioned toward the prosecution table, "Please continue, Ms. Cooper."

"I have no further questions, Your Honor."

"Very well. Mr. Morton, do you wish to cross?"

"I do, Your Honor," Salty said as he rose and, upon reaching the podium, asked, "Sgt. Bridges, do you have any evidence to refute the possibility that the victim had been stabbed before Ms. Zachary arrived on the scene?"

Cooper was livid. "OBJECTION," she shouted as she jumped from her chair knocking it over.

"State the nature of your objection, Ms. Cooper. The court cannot rule unless you state the grounds for your objection."

One of the deputies came forward and righted Cooper's chair. Cooper looked as though she was oblivious to the deputy's presence as she responded defiantly, "Calls for speculation and conjecture."

"Care to respond, Mr. Morton?" Judge Ralston asked as he turned in Salty's direction.

Salty stood and buttoned his suit jacket; he was ready with his response. "The charge itself is based on speculation or an unwarranted conclusion that my client inflicted the fatal wound. The prosecution is asking you to find probable cause based solely on the fact that she remained at the crime scene after calling 911 and was covered in blood after checking the victim's vital signs."

Cooper again was on her feet. "OBJECTION! There is no evidence the defendant got bloodied checking for vital signs."

"There is no evidence she got bloodied stabbing the victim either," Salty snapped back.

Judge Ralston leaned forward, and clasping his hands on the desk, peered down at the attorneys, "There…there. Both counsel need to restrain themselves! After all, there is no jury to impress here." After a moment of what appeared to Salty to be thoughtful reflection, the judge continued, "Ms. Cooper's objection as to assuming a fact not in evidence is sustained and the court will not consider defenses' contention that Ms. Zachery's bloodied appearance was caused from having checked the victim's vital signs. That having been said, the court finds that to infer the cause of the defendant's bloodied clothing is indeed speculation and conjecture."

Salty, with a hint of venom in his voice, said, "Isn't it just as much speculation and conjecture to conclude that Ms. Zachery must have stabbed the victim because when the police arrived she had blood on her hands?"

"Mr. Morton," Judge Ralston replied in a conciliatory tone, "the cause of the defendant's bloodied appearance is something for a jury to decide. The only issue before me today is whether there is probable cause, or reasonable grounds, to believe a crime was committed and that it was committed by your client."

Judge Ralston then said, "Mr. Morton, restate your original question and refrain from assuming facts not in evidence."

"Very well, Your Honor. Sgt. Bridges, would it be fair to say that Ms. Zachary not only called 911 but remained at the scene of the stabbing until the police arrived?"

"Yes," Sgt. Bridges replied as he nodded his head.

"Would it also be fair to say that when the police arrived, Ms. Zachary was cradling the victim's head in her hands and immersed in the victim's blood?" Salty persisted.

Again, Sgt. Bridges replied, "Yes."

"I take it, the victim was already deceased at the time the police arrived. Is that also correct?"

"Yes."

"What evidence did or do the police have that the victim was not deceased at the time Ms. Zachary arrived?"

"We don't know when Ms. Zachary arrived other than her statements."

Addressing Judge Ralston, Salty said, "The witness is being evasive and is not answering the question."

When Cooper arose to protest, Judge Ralston motioned for her to be seated. "The answer is indeed non-responsive," Judge Ralston said and turning to Sgt. Bridges admonished him to be responsive.

Defiantly, Sgt. Bridges replied, "Only circumstantial evidence."

"And what might that be?" Salty asked raising his eyebrows and tilting his head.

Sheepishly, Sgt. Bridges replied, "The defendant's bloody appearance…and, of course, the defendant's fingerprints on the murder weapon."

Salty started to say "No further questions" and instead, turning back in Sgt. Bridges' direction, said, "One further question, Sgt. Bridges. Obviously, you checked Ms. Zachary for wounds to see if she was involved in any kind of struggle. Did you see anything that would indicate that she was?"

Sgt. Bridges appeared pensive. Finally he said, "Other than her bloodied appearance and the fact that she was distraught, I detected nothing out of the ordinary."

"Thank you, Sgt. Bridges. We have no other questions of this witness," Salty said as he returned to the defense table.

Upon determining Cooper had no re-direct, Judge Ralston said, "Sgt. Bridges, you are excused."

When Jordan and Buddha later asked Salty why he hadn't questioned Bridges, about the alternate suspect, Salty replied, "The reason I opted not to mention the Carlton vehicle leaving the estates was because the time between when Jas saw the car and the time she found Nick would have to have been more than the two or three minutes the medical examiner noted in his report as to the time of Nick's death and would not be useful at this juncture and maybe not all."

At the end of the preliminary hearing, as expected, Judge Ralston found probable cause to bind the case over for trial. The parties then had to coordinate a date for trial along with deadlines for motions and/or other matters to be brought before the court. In the criminal justice system, the prosecution has a period of six months within which to commence the trial unless the defense waives speedy trial. Salty refused to waive speedy trial. He was convinced Jas was innocent or at the very least that there was no evidence to the contrary and he didn't want Jas to remain in jail longer than necessary, particularly since she was unable to make bond. She, of course, didn't have assets worth what was required to pay a bondsman $100,000 so she would, in all likelihood, remain in jail until the conclusion of the trial.

Jas was formally charged and advised on Wednesday July 24 and entered her plea of not guilty. The six-month speedy trial period began when Jas entered her not guilty plea and was calculated to run through January 24. The trial would have to commence prior to January 24.

Judge Ralston frowned at his calendar, cleared his throat and asked, "Gentlemen, how long do you anticipate the trial to last?"

Salty, leafing through the pages of his calendar, replied, "Your Honor, I will be filing motions, including a motion for change of venue. Depending on your rulings, it's hard to estimate a timeframe."

Special Prosecutor, Sylvia Cooper, concurred. "I think we should dispose of motions and other matters as soon a reasonably possible. The people will need at least four weeks to present their case...and, that's a rough estimate. We have an extensive list of witnesses including three experts that I anticipate calling."

Judge Ralston, consulting his calendar, said, "My only available block of time before the expiration of the six month period is during the holidays, November 10 through December 24. I had cordoned off that time for personal reasons but my plans can be rearranged."

Salty rubbed the bridge of his nose. *The judge probably planned to spend the holidays with his family. It's too bad he has to change plans but he's not the only one who must put Jas' welfare first.*

All parties agreed to the dates and so the trial of *The People of the State of New Mexico v. Jasmine Zachary* had been scheduled.

THE MOTIONS HEARING was scheduled for August 16. Salty filed motions for Change of Venue; Suppression of Physical Evidence; Suppression of Statements and other defense oriented motions. All, as expected, were summarily denied.

Although success at trial hinges on the success of pre-trial motions in most instances, Salty's resolve was not at all deterred. He was too much the professional to play Russian roulette and always had his ducks in a row no matter which way the ball bounced. The defense may have lost the battle but there was still a war to wage.

DURING THE PREPARATION of the case, Salty was haunted by Jas' statement that she saw the Carlton Realty car exit Nick's estate on several occasions.

Salty made daily visits to the detention facility to see Jas. On his next visit, he quizzed her further about seeing the Lexus. Looking thoughtful, she told him, "The newspaper ads for Carlton Realty usually include pictures of Adell and Winston. That's how I recognized her when I saw her leaving the Desert Rose Estates."

"Oh, of course. I remember seeing those ads myself." Salty replied, then tapping his fingertips together, he added, "However, that still doesn't explain why Adell Carlton was at the estates so often and presumably at McGregor's residence."

Jas just shook her head.

THE NEXT DAY, knowing it was probably a long shot, Salty said to Buddha, "I'd like you to interview Nick's neighbors and ascertain if any of them might have seen anything out of the ordinary or maybe even have seen the Carlton Realty Lexus at the crime scene on the afternoon of the murder. There is nothing in the police reports showing that any of the neighbors had been interviewed. The police apparently thought they had their man or more aptly their woman and didn't deem it necessary to look any further."

"The easy way out," Buddha muttered. "Sometimes it's just a matter of finding the most convenient scape-goat."

Salty didn't hear Buddha's response. He appeared to be in some distant place. He said in a soft voice to no one in particular, "After all, Jas was at the scene. Her fingerprints were found on the murder weapon as well as various objects throughout the house. She was covered with the victim's blood. Her DNA was lifted from utensils in the kitchen and various items in the bathrooms. She was the only person present during the time frame it took McGregor to die. It was an open-and-shut case. It was just that simple. No need to spend the time and expense hunting for an alternate suspect. The authorities' energies were best spent building a case against Jas. She was the only one who could have done it."

Buddha stood to leave. "I'm on it, Salty." Like a kid in the candy store, Buddha was eager to do the interviewing.

"Good. Keep me updated," Salty said and turned his attention back to the paperwork lying on his desk.

Buddha, wanting to get the lay of the land, rode his motorcycle along the back roads and skirted the Desert Rose Estates. Since most of the terrain was desert and there were no large trees or high fences to block the view, Buddha decided he would interview the neighbors on all four sides as they all had an open view of Nick's home and driveway.

The next day Buddha reported back to Salty. "I conducted a tour yesterday after I left here and scanned the McGregor neighborhood. It looks like all four of McGregor's immediate neighbors have a good view of the estate. I plan to surprise each of the neighbors so they don't have a chance to contrive a story or arrange not to be available."

"Excellent!" Salty said. Then looking Buddha over from head to toe, he said, "Buddha, I don't want you scaring young children and old women so could you trim that shaggy beard just a bit and look more like the brilliant investigator I know you to be. A different line of clothing would also help the total look; not that I have anything against worn, holey jeans and Harley T shirts but…."

Salty noticed the hurt look on Buddha's face as he replied, "Absolutely, Boss. However, I think your request transgresses into the realm of invasion of privacy and identity theft but, for you, the world."

"Ahh, I bet you say that to all your employers."

"Yeah, especially the ones who pay me."

10
SCATTERED SHOWERS

The next day Buddha began his quest and started with the neighbor's house to the east of Nick's estate. The name on the mailbox declared the residents to be "The Sanders." Buddha rang the doorbell which resounded the first few bars of *The March of the Wooden Soldiers*. "How quaint," he muttered to himself. A woman in her mid-50s answered the door with what Buddha would later describe as a violent jerk.

"Mrs. Sanders?"

"Yes. Sorry, we do not allow solicitors…"

"I'm not selling anything," Buddha proclaimed before she could close the door. "I'm investigating the murder of Nick McGregor. May I ask you a few questions?"

Mrs. Sanders looked as though she was relishing the thought of being involved in a murder investigation. She replied, "Oh, my, yes. I've been wondering when the police would get around to questioning me. Come in."

Buddha stepped into the foyer, "I'm not the police, I'm a private investigator. I was retained privately to try to fill in some gaps." Buddha thought he saw Mrs. Sanders stiffen so he rushed on before she could throw him out. "You appear to be a very observant person. Perhaps on the day of the murder, you noticed something unusual?"

Mrs. Sanders seemed to swell at the compliment. She answered, "Well, no, nothing unusual. Just the same old routine. One woman comes to visit and as soon as she leaves, another one shows up."

Buddha felt he had stumbled onto something, "Could you be more specific?"

Mrs. Sanders went to the door which was still open and pointed in the direction of the McGregor estate. "Of course. I have a splendid view of Nick's driveway. Here, take a look," and she stepped aside allowing Buddha to peer out the door.

"Yes, you certainly do," he said and smiled. "Please continue."

"Well, several times a week a realty lady driving a silver Lexus arrives at Nick's in the early afternoon. I wondered if Nick was buying, selling or trading real estate as often as the visits occurred. Then after the realty lady leaves, almost immediately that sweet little Jas shows up. Jas worked for Nick, you know, doing some redecorating."

Buddha nodded his head. "Yes. Go on."

"It was purely accidental that Jas and I met at the mailboxes occasionally. We visited a bit and, well, to be honest, I just don't believe she could have killed him."

"Why not?" Buddha asked.

"She certainly could not have overpowered him and besides she didn't appear to be the type to do something like that," Mrs. Sanders said with authority in her voice.

"Un-huh." Buddha looked past Mrs. Sanders at the luxurious appointments of the interior of the house and asked, "Did you see either the realty lady or Jas the afternoon Nick was murdered?"

Mrs. Sanders looked over her shoulder apparently wondering what Buddha was looking at. "Yes, I saw them both."

Paydirt! "Tell me about what you saw," Buddha prompted hoping the excitement in his voice wouldn't deter Mrs. Sanders' rendition of what she observed.

Apparently, Mrs. Sanders was concentrating on her narration and probably didn't notice Buddha's reaction. She said rather smugly, "Well, I recall about eleven in the morning I saw the Lexus going up the drive and then, when I looked out about an hour later, I observed it was still there. I went out to water my roses just about that time and saw the Lexus coming down Nick's drive. It had barely turned onto the main drag when I saw Jas come into view and turn into Nick's driveway. That was around twelve, twelve-thirty."

"Did you see anyone else besides the two women that afternoon?"

Mrs. Sanders said in an indignant tone, "No, I don't continuously stare out the window so there could have been other visitors that I wouldn't have noticed. But I did see both the realty lady and Jas."

Buddha asked in a more conciliatory tone, "Do you think you would recognize the realty lady if you saw her again?"

"Of course. I saw her come and go several times a week for months."

"Can you describe her to me?" Buddha asked hopefully.

Mrs. Sanders furrowed her brow looking thoughtful, "Well, she's short and lumpy…"

"Lumpy? What do you mean by 'lumpy'?"

"You know. She has large breasts and an ample rear which, on such a short frame, makes her look lumpy. H-u-m-m, not too attractive either, dingy unkempt straight blond hair." Mrs. Sanders looked perplexed as she said, "I wondered what Nick saw in her. She just didn't seem his type. His deceased wife was movie star beautiful, if you know what I mean."

"Yes, I've seen pictures of her and I do know what you mean." Trying to keep Mrs. Sanders on track, Buddha asked, "How long did the realty lady's visits usually last?"

"About an hour; sometimes more, sometimes less."

"And you're sure she was there the day of the murder?"

"Yes, I'm absolutely positive."

"Would you be willing to testify to that if need be?"

Mrs. Sanders' eyes suddenly brightened, "Oh, my yes."

Buddha nodded. After a moment he asked, "Is there anything else you can add, anything at all?"

Mrs. Sanders slowly shook her head and murmured "No. Can't think of anything."

"Thank you for your time, Mrs. Sanders. Here's my card. If you do think of anything else, even if you think it might not be useful, it may be, please call me."

"Oh, I will. Do you think I'll be called to testify?"

"At this stage, I can't say. However your willingness to do so goes a long way. We'll be in touch."

BUDDHA, HAVING BEEN encouraged by his first interview, proceeded to the neighbor on the west. The mailbox didn't announce who lived there so he had to wing it. A mousy man, probably in his late 60s answered the door.

Buddha put on, what he thought was, his most charming smile, "Good afternoon, Sir. I'm Dave Jennings," Buddha said as he fished a card from his shirt pocket. "I've been employed to investigate the murder of Nick McGregor..."

BAM! The door slammed almost hitting Buddha in the face. He jumped back and, as he did so, he stumbled from the portico landing hard on the bottom step. After a moment, he arose and dusting his off his khakis muttered, "I've got to work on my charm."

BUDDHA JAMMED HIS hands into his pants' pockets and walked back to the street. Standing by the open door of his Rover, he reached in and retrieved his sun glasses from the dash. He looked at the remaining two houses, he finally decided to try the house to the north. *Hope they don't sic the dogs on me or fill my already bruised butt full of buckshot.*

Buddha stood examining the black wrought iron lion's head knocker. Still stinging, not so much from pain but dejection, Buddha stepped back a few paces after knocking. Soon a maid opened the massive mahogany door a crack and peered out. Buddha blinked. *This is the stuff dreams are made of.* The almost perfect-in-every-way maid was dressed in the traditional short black dress/white apron uniform, albeit without the feather duster in her hand.

"Yes?" she said without smiling.

"Hello. I'm Dave Jennings." Buddha pushed his card through the slit in the door.

The door remained unchanged as the maid examined the card.

Buddha tilted his head peering through the crack, "How are you today, Ms…?" he asked awkwardly.

"Sophia. My name is Sophia and I'm well, thank you," she replied and Buddha thought he detected a twinkle in her eye.

"Sophia! That's a lovely name. Is it French?"

Sophia opened the door a few more inches, "Heavens, no! I was named after an Italian actress."

"But I thought I detected a French accent when you spoke."

"If you did, you'd be the first. I grew up in Santa Fe." Sophia smiled broadly. "Do you have business with the Elmingtons?"

Buddha put his hand on the doorjamb and leaned forward peering inside. He said, "Not necessarily. I'm investigating the McGregor murder and canvassing the neighborhood to ascertain if anyone had seen anything suspicious on the day he was killed."

Sophia nodded her head but held her ground. "I've been expecting someone to question us ever since the murder took place. The Elmingtons are out for the day but I'd be happy to tell you what I know."

Pay dirt! Buddha then asked "May I come in?"

"Yes." Then, before she stepped back allowing him entry, she said, "But first you must remove your shoes and leave them by the door."

"I must?" Buddha asked looking down at his feet.

"You must!"

Grudgingly, Buddha complied, somewhat embarrassed by the hole in one sock that was glaringly apparent. When he entered the mansion, he was awestruck by the elaborate motif and the enormity of the interior. Sophia, amused at his reaction, said, "Quit gawking and follow me to the kitchen." He blushed and was grateful she hadn't caught him gawking at *her* eye catching appointments. Redirecting his gaze, Buddha padded along behind Sophia in his stocking feet.

Once he was seated at the marble top counter with a glass of ice tea she had provided, Sophia asked in a chirpy voice, "So, what is it you want to know?"

Buddha resisted the urge to say your phone number. Instead he said, "It's been rumored that a silver Lexus had been seen at Nick's house quite often and was there the afternoon he was murdered." Looking into Sophia's lovely brown eyes over the top of his glass, he took a sip of tea, he continued, "I know you must keep very busy here but on the off-chance you might have..."

"Funny that you mention it," Sophia interrupted, tapping her fingers on the counter. "Of course. I couldn't help but notice the comings and goings at Nick's." She laughed and looked a little embarrassed, saying, "I even started keeping a record of the women in-and-out because I suspected, having that many female visitors, it was just a matter of time before something happened."

Buddha had discovered a witness who had kept score. He gulped and choked as he swallowed his drink of tea.

Sophia ran around the counter and began patting him on the back.

"Are you all right?" she asked with panic in her voice.

Buddha, unable to talk, just nodded as he waved her off. When the coughing spell subsided, he wiped the tears from his eyes and said, "Sorry I frightened you." Then he took a deep breath in an effort to quiet his excitement and said in as calm of a voice as he could muster, "Please tell me what you saw that day."

Sophia clicked her tongue. "In my opinion, Nick was quite the gigolo."

"That so?"

"My God! Are you kidding, the jerk had two women who were regulars and no telling how many others on the side."

"How do you know that?" Buddha crossed his arms on the counter and leaned toward Sophia.

Sophia adjusted her apron and sat back down. "I noticed others come and go but never regularly. That was before the pretty auburn haired woman appeared on the scene." Sophia, looking thoughtful, continued, "I believe she is the one charged with his murder." Then her face darkened, "He probably deserved it! After auburn hair started visiting, all others ceased except for the real estate woman. She would show up early in the afternoon and leave just before auburn-hair drove up. She would drive out on cue as if she had received some kind of mysterious signal or order to get the hell out." Sophia smiled a sly smile, "I often wondered what Nick would do if the two of them met in his driveway."

Buddha returned the smile. *This little vixen has a mean streak.* He then looked around, "H-m-m-m, your line of vision from here appears to be pretty limited?"

Sophia stood. "Come with me and I'll show you." She then led him up the massive spiral staircase. She motioned him into a bedroom at the front of the house and pointed to a window overlooking the estates with a view of the entire neighborhood. Some front views; some back views.

Walking Buddha to a large window, Sophia drew back the gossamer curtains. She gestured to the home directly across from the Elmington's mansion. "That's Nick's place."

The view was a side view of the back patio and the entire driveway. Buddha's heart stopped for a second. He drew in a quick breath and exhaled loudly. "So I see. Please, go on."

There was an air of authority in Sophia's voice as she continued. "Since it was the weekend, the routine was different."

Sophia turned and leaned against the window sill looking at Buddha. "Auburn hair would usually arrive earlier. That weekend, however, the Elmingtons had out-of-town guests who were here for the annual tribal pow-wow summer festival. The front bedroom was being occupied by one of the guests. Late that afternoon I took fresh towels up, and as I tidied up the room, I glanced out but I didn't see anyone arrive or leave. I did notice Nick was bar-b-queuing and seemed to be talking to someone inside.

Sophia turned her head and looked out of the window. "Upon arrival, the cars park out of my line of vision so, unless I see them arrive, I don't always know whose there." She looked back at Buddha, "Later in the evening we heard sirens and went outside to see what was happening. You know the rest, I assume."

Buddha nodded. "You said you kept a journal."

"Yes, I have it in my room downstairs."

"May I take it and make a copy?" he asked.

"Absolutely, if you think it would help. But, I do want it back."

"Yes, of course. And, I believe it will be of enormous value in establishing that Nick had other visitors besides the one charged with his murder."

"Come on," Sophia said as she led Buddha back to the foyer. "Wait here, I'll get my journal."

When she returned she handed a neat leather bound book to Buddha. Glancing through the journal, Buddha said,

"Although you didn't know the names of the visitors, recording the vehicle make and color was a stroke of genius."

Sophia smiled broadly as she opened the door indicating it was time for Buddha to leave. He stepped out and slipped into his shoes.

"Thank you for the tea. Your observations and journal, I believe, will be very helpful."

Sophia looked pleased as she replied, "You're welcome."

"Please call if you remember anything else. I'll return the journal as soon as possible. We would request that you keep it in a safe place in case we need to enter it as evidence at trial."

"Yes, I will." Sophia waved goodbye as Buddha walked to his Range Rover.

BUDDHA CHECKED HIS watch, ten forty-five. He still had time to interview the neighbors to the south. The interviewees may not be too friendly if he interrupted their lunch. The name on the mailbox announced this was "The Shipleys" residence. Buddha, buoyed by two positive interviews, walked briskly to the front door. A "No Solicitors Allowed" sign was positioned on the front portico in a place where it could not be missed. When Buddha rang, the door was opened by a small boy wearing thick pop-bottle type glasses.

"Can't you read?" the boy demanded.

Buddha, ignoring the boy's bad manners, said, "Hi, my name is Dave. Yes, I saw the sign but I'm not selling anything." Then looking past the boy into the foyer, he asked, "Is your mother or father home?"

"Why?"

"I would like to speak to them."

"Why?"

Buddha was becoming exasperated. "It's grownup business. Please let me please speak with your parents."

The boy shrank back into the foyer and called, "Mom, some freaky looking guy wants to talk to you."

Much to Buddha's relief, the boy's mother appeared, wiping her hands belligerently on her apron. "If you're selling," she said briskly, "we don't want any."

"Mrs. Shipley, forgive me for interrupting you. I'm a private investigator," Buddha said handing her his card, "I'm interviewing Nick McGregor's neighbors to determine if anyone noticed anything unusual the day he was murdered."

Directing her attention to her offspring, Mrs. Shipley said sharply, "Malcolm, go watch your cartoons while I talk to this man." Then to Buddha she snapped, "How can I help?"

Glad I'm not this bitch's son. "Thank you for your time, Mrs. Shipley. Anything you observed would be useful. I notice you have a fairly good view of the McGregor estate from here. I know how busy you must be with a child and big home to care for but perhaps you did notice..."

Mrs. Shipley interrupted Buddha and snarled, "You're absolutely correct! I am very busy, especially right now. We are having a dinner party and there's much to do." A look of anguish crossed her face as she continued, "That damn catering service misplaced my order and now I have to do it all. Oh, never mind. I didn't see anything out of the ordinary and if I had, I would already have told the police. So, if you'll excuse me..."

"Yes, of course." Buddha knew when he was getting the bum's rush and decided not to pursue the conversation. "Thank you again for your time. You have my card if you..."

"Yes, yes." She snarled, "Good afternoon." Mrs. Shipley then slammed the door. Buddha instinctively jumped backward. He later told Salty he thought he should be entitled to hazardous duty pay.

11
UNSEASONABLY WARM

As Buddha drove back to Salty's office, he was thinking of his 500 batting average. Not too shabby considering his team was in the cellar only hours before.

When he arrived, Jordan asked, "How'd it go?"

When Buddha answered, Jordan detected a smugness in his tone, "We'll see what you think after I prepare my report. Will you type it for me?"

"Well, of course," Jordan agreed. "Don't I always?" Jordan then made a display of loosening up her fingers by lacing them together and stretching out her arms. Buddha just rolled his eyes knowing she was making fun of him.

She typed in tandem with his dictation. When they got to the Elmington maid's interview, Jordan exclaimed, "Oh, my God, you hit a home run."

Buddha swelled, "Yeah, that's exactly what I thought."

"Do you have the journal?" Jordan asked with excited anticipation.

"Yep, right here," and he held it up for Jordan to see. When she reached for it, he jerked it back holding it just out of her reach. She jumped up and began to playfully scuffle with Buddha attempting to get her hands on the journal. "Easy, woman! This could be an important piece of evidence," Buddha cautioned.

Just then Salty arrived back at the office. "What's going on?" he demanded.

Jordan turned and smoothing her hair, sat back down at her desk. "Oh, nothing. We were just messing around."

Buddha winked at Salty.

"You two act like a couple of teenagers." Then turning his attention to Buddha, Salth asked, "How'd it go?"

Buddha brought Salty up to speed. Upon hearing the details of the morning's expedition, Salty was more encouraged, excited and enthused than he had been since he took on the case.

"Jordan, after you complete Buddha's report, please prepare a Defendant's Additional Witness List including all four of McGregor's neighbors."

Jordan nodded.

"I have to go back to court this afternoon so I'll file it then," Salty remarked. Retreating towards his office he turned and said, "Good work, Buddha. Your interviews will certainly be a big help, in fact, they may make our case." Then looking at Jordan, he said, "Carry on!"

EVEN THOUGH THE trial was months away, Salty began prepping. As he examined the reports and evidence, he would jot down items as they occurred to him so that they didn't get lost in the maze. Means, motive and opportunity would be the crux of his defense, especially motive. *What motive would Jas have had for killing Nick?* This question still haunted him and perhaps always would.

At some point Salty would have to interview the neighbors in person and decide whose testimony would best benefit his client. Of course, by listing all of the neighbors as witnesses, the prosecution would also have a crack at them. This did not trouble Salty if the two good witnesses were telling the truth and stuck to their story. He also felt the prosecution would get the same warm reception from the two uncooperative neighbors who had given Buddha the blistering brush-off.

SALTY SPENT MANY hours with Jas going over her story. He never detected any deceit in her rendition. He resolved he would ask SP Cooper why their investigation hadn't extended to Nick's neighbors. *Is the prosecution so sure that Jas is the culprit that they don't need to look for alternate suspects?*

He would tell Cooper about the Carlton Realty involvement and see if he could exact a promise of further investigation. He also knew from the discovery that there were two separate sets of muddy tire tracks that had been photographed. Also multiple DNA samples that had been collected, as well as a variety of fingerprints. He would like to get a non-testimonial identification order from the court ordering the collection of DNA samples and fingerprints from Adell Carlton and her husband/partner, Winston Carlton. That might be tricky if the prosecution bowed its neck and objected to the issuing of the order. He would ask Cooper in advance if the prosecution had an objection to the process. Surely the prosecution was as anxious as he to bring the perpetrator to justice and not risk convicting an innocent person, namely Jas.

THE NEXT DAY Salty called the Albuquerque DA's office to make an appointment with Cooper.

"Mr. Morton, what can I do for you?" Cooper asked without a formal greeting.

"Good morning, Ms. Cooper. This is a curtesy call to inform you that I'm in the process of filing a motion for non-testimonial identification to be collected from Adell and Winston Carlton." After a slight pause, he asked, "Do you have any objection?"

"Well, since I don't even know who these people are, who knows?"

"In a nutshell, I had my investigator interview McGregor's neighbors and the Carlton name came up during those interviews. Apparently, Adell Carlton was seen frequently at the McGregor estate."

"I see. And what kind of evidence are you seeking?"

"Fingerprints and DNA."

"DNA?" *What does he know that I don't?* Cooper told Salty, "I'll be in Farmington on Monday. Can we meet sometime in the afternoon?"

"Of course. Say," Salty consulted his calendar, "around three?"

"Affirmative. In the meantime, go ahead and file your motion." *I need to get Bridges on this. How is it they failed to interview the neighbors? Dammit anyway!*

Salty had Jordan prepare the appropriate document and he filed it with the court. When it was signed by Judge Ralston, the clerk forwarded copies to law enforcement with instructions to collect samples of DNA and fingerprints from the Carltons. Salty and Cooper also received signed copies of the order so they knew the process had been initiated and they could incorporate whatever the results revealed into their respective cases. They both knew normally it could take weeks to get the results. However, since this was a capital case and speedy trial was running, the lab would expedite the analysis and place this case close to the top, if not at the top, of the list.

AFTER MUCH CONSIDERATION, Salty decided to play his trump card and have Buddha interview the Carlton woman. She would already be on notice from being served with the non-testimonial identification order. He knew it was a long shot and would probably alert her that she was being considered as a suspect, if not by law enforcement then by the defense.

Buddha, with pen and pad in hand, entered the Carlton Realty office. The office was spacious and elaborately styled with expensive furniture and artwork signifying an air of pomposity and prosperity.

Buddha, approaching the reception desk handed his business card to the mature but attractive receptionist. The nameplate on her desk identified her as Renee Hanson.

"Good afternoon, Ms. Hanson."

"Good afternoon, Mr…" Renee paused and looked at the card Buddha had handed her, "Mr. Jennings. What can I do for you?"

Buddha looked around before answering, "I'd like to see Mrs. Carlton if she's available."

"If you'll take a seat, I'll check," Renee squinted up at him and picked up the telephone.

Buddha opted not sit down and kept his gaze on the receptionist. Renee shifted nervously under his scrutiny. Finally, one of the two office doors opened and Adell Carlton briskly walked toward Buddha. She extended her hand in greeting and gestured toward her open door, saying, "Please come in and have a seat."

Oops, she probably thinks I'm a client looking for property.

Jas' description of a "short, dumpy woman with stringy dishwater blond hair" was dead on. Buddha also noticed Sophia had nailed her as well but Sophia had been more than generous in labeling her not too attractive. BINGO!

"Well, Mr. Jennings," Adell said as she sat down and adjusted her skirt, "how can we help you? That is, what kind of property are you looking for?"

"Mrs. Carlton, I'm not looking for property. I'm here seeking answers to some lingering questions surrounding the McGregor murder." Buddha noticed Carlton's quick intake of breath and sudden change of facial expression. What he did not know was that the two offices of the Carlton's were connected on an intercom system so that each could hear what was transpiring in the other. As the two spoke, Buddha was unaware Winston Carlton was listening in his office with piqued curiosity.

"Why, I'm not sure I know anything that would be of use," Adell said nervously intertwining her fingers together on the desk in front of her and glancing in the direction of the adjacent office.

Buddha leaned back and crossed his legs, "I have witnesses who will testify that they saw your car at the McGregor residence the afternoon of the murder." He watched Adell stiffen in her chair. "They will also testify your car was a regular at Nick's and that they observed you being there in the early afternoon on many occasions including the day he was murdered. Can you explain…"

Adell's face became a pinched mask of horror. She was quick to respond. Buddha also noticed her voice was laced with fear, "Well, I never! They're lying, of course. I was not there that day nor was I *ever* at his house."

Adell's denial reminded Buddha of a former president denying a romantic affair and using words to that effect. He leaned forward and asked, "Did you have other business at the Desert Rose Estates?"

"Perhaps." Adell took a few moments and then added, "Our business takes us all over San Juan County. I really couldn't say where I was the afternoon of the murder, except that I wasn't there."

Buddha stood his ground and asked, "Are you the only one that drives the silver Lexus?"

"No, Winston also drives it on occasion."

OVERHEARING HIS WIFE'S feeble denial, Winston's heart sank. He knew Adell was not faithful but he had always turned a blind eye. Now he was hit smack between the eyes with it and had to face the facts. "Oh, Adell," he whispered, "my dear, sweet darling." Quite obviously Winston was still very much in love with Adell despite her philandering. *Whatever would I do without you if you did this and were convicted?*

As Winston sat there listening to the conversation, a plan began formulating in his mind.

Although Adell was now not the beauty Winston first fell in love with, she was still his only love. Soon after they were married, she began to let herself slip. She put on weight and didn't take as much pride in her appearance as she had before.

Winston found that he missed her physical beauty but he wouldn't trade her for *Venus*. He began reminiscing about when he and Adell first met. She was really something back then. She was lovely. Her figure was the envy of all the women and the fantasy of all the men. She was careful about her appearance and had her hair styled weekly. Her makeup was designed by a Hollywood cosmetologist.

Adell had captivated his heart although he was twenty years older than she. The two fell in love and married. Together they successfully built Carlton Realty into a major money making machine. That is, until the crash hit in the mid-2000s. When the stock market slowed down, the Carltons were well protected because Adell was a financial genius and a had knack for investing. Even when times were hard she continued to invest wisely and made money.

Winston, now in his late seventies was not in the best of health. He realized that his life-span was short and unpredictable. He was no longer able to enjoy sex, had to watch his diet, had so many aches and pains he couldn't even list them all. His lack of energy and the onset of old age in general kept him from doing things he had so thoroughly relished just a few years before such as golfing, boating and tennis. Even travelling was becoming tiresome. Adell, however, now in her fifties was still vibrant and enjoying life and why shouldn't she? She had given him so much pleasure during their time together he couldn't even conceive of life without her.

Sitting there at his desk with his head buried in his crossed arms, Winston suspected Adell did have something to do with the murder. He had engaged in some recon work on his own and had spotted her car in McGregor's driveway on numerous occasions. He knew Adell to have a quick and sometimes violent temper so it wouldn't surprise him if she was the one that plunged the knife into McGregor. Musing over these things, Winston knew losing her would be a death sentence for him. He decided at that moment that he would intervene if Adell was charged and brought to trial. He would confess to the murder and sacrifice himself to spare her if necessary. If he lost her he would have nothing left to live for anyway.

BUDDHA CONTINUED TO question Adell. "Did you know the victim, Nick McGregor?"

"Yes, I knew him." Adell fidgeted, looking as though she was trying to avoid any further comment.

"How did you know him?"

"I remember him from my school days. He had graduated years before I entered high school but he was still considered a Farmington High icon. He was quite the athlete and always featured in the local newspaper's sports page." Adell looked at the ceiling apparently recalling those days. "The school trophy case is full of trophies that Nick had won or helped win for the Cougars. I understand he lived with his family in Albuquerque and worked for World Wide Airlines. His parents lived here and he visited often, or so the society section of the *Farmington Times* reported."

Buddha nodded but remained silent. Adell was on a roll and he wanted her to continue uninterrupted.

"His parents were very active in the church. They were featured in the newspaper from time-to-time, sometimes with pictures of Nick and his family. After his parents were killed, they, Nick and his family, moved back to Farmington to the family estate. That is pretty much all I really know about the McGregors and Nick in particular."

"Un-huh." Buddha's voice brimmed with rancor as he asked, , "Then, tell me, how do you explain your car being seen at Nick's so often?"

Adell was on her feet. She shouted, "I DON'T HAVE TO EXPLAIN THAT BECAUSE IT NEVER HAPPENED. HOW MANY TIMES DO I HAVE TO TELL YOU THAT? Perhaps I should call my lawyer."

Buddha snarled, "That's up to you. I'm just trying to piece together some loose ends in an effort to arrive at the truth."

Adell placed her palms flat on her desk, and hissed, "I'm not answering any more of your ridiculous questions. This conversation is over. Get out! NOW!."

At that moment, Winston barged into Adell's office. "Oh, excuse me, I didn't know you were busy. Remember, we have an appointment and we're already late. Are you able to get away now?"

"Yes, you bet. We're done here." Adell marched to the door and flung it open. "Good day, Mr. Jennings."

Buddha relished taunting people, especially when their anger was out of control. He rose and said in his most patronizing voice, "Thank you for your time. I'll be in touch."

"I certainly hope not." Adell said as she slammed the door behind him.

Buddha left the realty office knowing in his heart that Adell was lying. He wanted to pursue the matter further but would have to confer with Salty and get permission to do some real detective work on his own.

ONCE BUDDHA WAS gone, Winston sat down across from Adell and asked, "What was that all about?"

Adell narrowed her eyes as she answered, "Oh, some busy bodies thought they saw my car at the Desert Rose Estates on the same day Nick McGregor was murdered."

"Did they?"

Adell answered in a huff, "I categorically deny ever being there, much less on that day. Dammit, now don't you start. I've had all I can take for one day. Besides, I assume you were in your office and overheard our entire conversation."

Winston let the matter drop. His plan was in place and there was no use evoking Adell's ire. He was already relegated to the spare bedroom in the basement.

12
BELOW FREEZING

December first was a bitter cold, intensely windy day in Farmington. Yet, despite the weather, the courtroom was packed to capacity. Salty reasoned that from the public's interest in the trial and the expansive media coverage, if it came to it, he would appeal the denial of his change of venue motion and request a trial be held in another city that wasn't quite as saturated with coverage. There were no guarantees the appeal would be granted but at least it could fall under the category of "Plan B."

Since Nick and Jas were both residents of Farmington, public curiosity was much more intense than what it would have been otherwise. They both had a multitude of local friends. Jas owned and operated her own very successful business on Main Street and knew just about everyone in Farmington. She was on the boards of the Better Business Bureau and Chamber of Commerce.

Nick was a retired World Wide pilot and a local celebrity of some stripe. Both were active in the Catholic Church as well as community organizations. Thus, the interest in this particular trial was overwhelming. It appeared there wasn't a soul in Farmington who hadn't heard of the trial of the century and the gallery was anxiously waiting for it to begin.

JAS, LOOKING VERY thin and drawn, sat between Salty and Buddha at the defense table. The five months she spent incarcerated awaiting trial had taken its toll. She had no spare fat to begin with but managed to lose fifteen pounds anyway. Yvonne, who was in touch with her as much as the jail allowed, bought Jas appropriate clothing for trial, and now wearing a black pants suit and white blouse, Jas seemed unaware that she was the center of attention. Her hair had lost its luster and she was makeup-free except for some lip gloss which she applied to help ease her dry lips.

Salty sat quietly beside her. *Despite everything she has been through, she's still stunning.* Something stirred inside him and he suddenly realized how much he was attracted to her–clearly beyond the bounds of attorney/client relationship. *Could I be falling in love with her?*

THE COURT CLERK looked back when she heard the door between the courtroom and chambers open. She said, "All rise." Judge Ralston entered the courtroom and took his seat on the bench. Salty felt Jas jerk when the judge entered. He squeezed her hand and whispered, "Calm down. It's going to be all right." Jas seemed to relax.

The judge held up his hands and motioned for all to be seated. Pushing his glasses up, he perused the file on his desk. He then nodded to his clerk and she announced the name of the case at bar, *People of the State of New Mexico v. Jasmine Zachary.*

The judge peered over his glasses at the attorneys, "Are we ready to proceed?"

Both sides said they were.

The grueling task of selecting a jury commenced. It dragged on for almost a full week just as anticipated. Each prospective juror was basically asked the same questions or indiscernible variations thereof. To say it was boring to on-lookers was an understatement. However, to the participants, selecting the right jurors to sit in judgment was as paramount to winning the case as was the case itself. The defense and prosecution paid close attention to the answers to the various questions as well as the demeanor of the responding jurors. By noon on Friday, the fifth day of jury selection, the parties had agreed on the panel and the judge swore the prospective jurors in.

Salty was neither hot nor cold on the group as a whole but liked several who he thought would weigh the evidence and return a fair verdict. A fair verdict, in his eyes, of course, was a verdict of not guilty.

The panel consisted of seven women and five men of various ages and two alternates, both women. Salty was pleased that there were more women than men for obvious reasons. He felt the women, for example, would be more sympathetic to Jas given the circumstances and Nick's social history.

By the time the ritual was completed it was 1:30 p.m. Judge Ralston recessed court until the following Monday.

Before he excused the jurors, he said, "You are instructed not to read, listen to or view anything in the media or discuss or listen to discussions pertaining to the trial. You cannot discuss it with anyone, not even your spouse."

Then looking at the attorneys, he said, "After opening statements, the prosecution will be called upon to present its case-in-chief." It was postured more as a demand rather than a statement. The implication was that he would tolerate no continuances or delays.

Cooper stood and said, "Yes, Your Honor, we will be ready." Then as a curtesy, she stated, "We will call our expert witnesses first, law enforcement personnel next and then the lay witnesses. Our presentation consists of a total of nine witnesses."

"Thank you, Ms. Cooper." Then, looking stern, Ralston informed the attorneys, "Each side will be allowed only one hour to make an opening statement."

It was legendary that Ralston was a strict enforcer of *his rules* and attorneys who appeared before him were often made painfully aware of his disdain for those who disregarded his mandates.

MONDAY, JANUARY 14, was ushered in with the predicated heavy snow storm which made traveling from place-to-place in Farmington difficult. Farmington's road department was still painfully pitiful and had not improved much since last year's Christmas storm. Nonetheless, the courtroom was packed with spectators. Salty, having to use the visitor's parking lot was annoyed at how carelessly people had parked their cars because of their inability to see the lines dividing the parking spaces. He made a pass through the lot, but then decided to park on the street to avoid the hodge-podge environment created within the parking lot. The one and only snow plow had plowed the streets surrounding the courthouse in anticipation of heavy traffic due to the trial.

Salty, arriving early was fortunate enough to get a parking spot on the street close to the front entrance. The city had placed bags over the parking meters proclaiming it was not necessary to pay on this day due to weather conditions. *Well, things are looking up. Perhaps the rest of the day will be as amiable.*

Special Prosecutor Cooper was seated at the prosecution table rifling through a stack of files. Seated next to her was second chair, Deputy District Attorney Dan Williams. Cooper gingerly pulled a page from a file and placed it in front of her just as Salty approached.

Salty said, "Good morning. I trust you had a pleasant weekend here in Farmington. We don't usually get this much snow. Did you order it?"

Cooper replied, "If I had that kind of pull, I'd be in a different line of work which would necessarily include reclining on a distant sunny beach somewhere warm and tropical." They all laughed good-naturedly and Salty crossed the aisle to set up shop at the defense table. After pulling out his work-product, he put his briefcase on the floor next to him. Buddha, who was already seated at the defense table, was dressed court appropriate and had his beard trimmed to a respectable length.

The door leading to the holding area opened and Salty and Buddha looked up. Jas was being led in by a burly sheriff's deputy. After she was seated, the sheriff's deputy retreated back to the holding area door and stood there alert and militarily erect. Since this was a high-profile case, more than the usual number of deputies were assigned courtroom duty and were strategically positioned throughout to maintain the peace and dignity of the court as mandated by Judge Ralston.

Salty whispered to Jas, "I feel we have a decent jury and our case is solid. We have more than a fighting chance. Try to relax and not look so tense. Jurors notice every detail and their interpretation may not be accurate." Then he gave Jas a searching look and said, "Incidentally, you look very nice."

Jas smiled up at him and he squeezed her hand. Buddha touched her arm in a supportive gesture. The defense team was ready, more than ready, they were rearing to go.

JUDGE RALSTON LOOKING up from the sheets of paper spread before him raised his eyebrows and asked, "Are the parties ready to proceed?"

"Yes, Your Honor," both defense and prosecution answered in unison.

"Very well, then, we will hear opening statements. Remember, you're each restricted to one hour. Ms. Cooper, you may proceed."

With a practiced motion, Cooper rose and circled the prosecution's table, saying, "Thank you, Your Honor." She was now at the podium, "Good morning ladies and gentlemen. Thank you for venturing out on such a cold winter day to serve on this jury. We know the personal sacrifice you make by serving on a lengthy trial and we truly appreciate your willingness to do so."

Cooper stepped from behind the podium, closed the gap between her and the jury and continued, "Opening statements are designed to acquaint the jury in broad strokes with what the parties intend to prove. They are the skeleton of the case, if you will, and will then be filled in with facts as the case proceeds through the trial process.

"We, the people, intend to prove to you beyond a reasonable doubt that the defendant in this case, Jasmine Zachary, also known as Jas Zachary, is indeed the perpetrator of the murder of Nicholas McGregor." Cooper looked sharply at Jas and returned to the podium. Once in position, she held up a bound report, "The evidence will show that no one else could have committed the act. The defendant was found cradling the victim at the scene of the crime soaked in his blood; her fingerprints were on the murder weapon; her DNA was found on the recently used unwashed dishes in the kitchen; her DNA was also found on bathroom items such as combs and toothbrushes; her fingerprints were scattered throughout the villa in various rooms; and, her bathing suit and some personal items were found in a guest bedroom in the mansion."

Cooper took a sip of water and continued, "The evidence will show that the victim did not die instantly of a stab wound. He bled to death because of that wound. Our expert witness, Forensic Pathologist Walter Grasso, will testify as to the time frame within which it takes a man the size of the victim to bleed to death after suffering a wound similar to the one inflicted on the victim. The expert's estimate of the time frame is not long, two or three minutes.

"Furthermore, according to the defendant herself," Cooper turned toward Jas again and pointed, "she was the only person at the crime scene during the time estimated for the victim to die as stated in the forensic pathologist's report. If another person had committed the crime and made an escape before the defendant arrived on the scene, the victim would have surly been dead, albeit within a minute or so, before discovery of the body. The defendant also stated she detected shallow breathing when she arrived and immediately called 911. Of course, the defendant is not a medical doctor but which one of us could not detect shallow breathing? One, of course, doesn't have to have an MD behind his or her name to see a person's chest rise and fall."

Cooper circled the podium again, and paused a moment for effect. Then she continued, "There is a lengthy driveway leading to the victim's mansion. By the time the killer did the deed, exited the house and got to his or her car, a substantial number of those two or three minutes would have elapsed. Additionally, it is not likely that the two vehicles would have passed in the driveway, each undetected by the other if another person was leaving as the defendant arrived. The evidence will show that the driveway is the only viable way in and the only viable way out."

Cooper went on and on well into the allotted hour regaling the jury with the prosecution's case-in-chief. Most of her commentary was repeating what she had previously said with little variation and expounding on her experts' expected testimony. After what seemed like an eternity, she concluded by stating, "The People, the side I represent, will erase any reasonable doubt you may have regarding the guilt of the defendant and, should the evidence warrant it, we will be requesting that you return a guilty verdict at the conclusion of the trial. Thank you."

After Cooper took her seat, Judge Ralston said, "We will now take a brief recess. Bailiff, please have the jurors back in fifteen minutes."

FIFTEEN MINUTES LATER Judge Ralston was back on the bench and court was reconvened. Without hesitation, the judge said, "Mr. Morton, you may proceed with your opening statement."

"Thank you, Your Honor," Salty said as he stood and buttoned his suit jacket. Approaching the podium, he said, "We, too, ladies and gentlemen thank you for your service." He then slid his hands into his pants pockets and walked around the podium toward the jury box, "I will be brief. I do not intend to put on our entire defense in my opening statement." Salty then paused and looked at each juror. "We will refute, even though the defense is not required to do so, all of the prosecution's claims that Ms. Zachary was the only person who could have committed the murder.

"Yes, she was there covered in the victim's blood but only because she was trying to save him. Her fingerprints were found on the murder weapon because she was trying to remove the knife in an effort to do all she could to help Mr. McGregor. Her DNA and fingerprints would naturally be found throughout the house because she spent a lot of time there working with Mr. McGregor on the remodel of his residence. She wasn't restricted to just a few rooms; the remodel included every room in the mansion. She was invited by Mr. McGregor to enjoy the pool and cool off during the hot New Mexico afternoons so, naturally, her swimsuit and other personal items would be present. As far as Ms. Zachary noticing 'shallow breathing,' that can be attributed to her state of mind in wanting him to be alive. It could also be attributed to her cradling him thus forcing air from of his lungs. Who knows how many scenarios could apply. How does all of this add up to her having committed the crime?"

Salty took a deep breath and paused to let his last statement sink in. He was now standing erect at the podium. "The evidence will show that the medical examiner's time frame is only an estimate or what one might call an educated guess; that could be wrong. Just by adding a couple of minutes, another person could have been present, committed the murder and fled before the defendant even turned into the driveway."

Salty turned toward Jas, "My client will testify even though she is not required to do so, that she passed another car just before she arrived at the McGregor driveway. There were two sets of muddy tire prints in the driveway. Where did the second set come from if there hadn't been another vehicle present immediately after the afternoon rain? The defense will prove to you that there is a reasonable doubt, even more than a reasonable doubt, that the defendant committed the crime with which she is charged.

"More important than the aforementioned, is evidence that the defendant had no motive for killing Mr. McGregor. There is a standard that is used in the legal profession, means, motive and opportunity. These are the three elements needed to sustain a conviction. The evidence will show the defendant had the means and the opportunity but no motive. The prosecution's opening statement was devoid of even a hint that the defendant had a motive for killing Mr. McGregor. She worked *for* him. The question is why would she want to eliminate an additional source of income? It just doesn't make sense. And, if she were guilty why wouldn't she have fled from the scene? The evidence will show that she not only stayed at the scene, but called 911 and feverishly tried to revive Mr. McGregor. Is that what a guilty person would do? Or, did Ms. Zachary do what an innocent person would have done?

"I'm positive that after all the evidence has been presented and all the witnesses have testified you, too, will be convinced my client is innocent.

"Your service as jurors is greatly appreciated and I know you will do the right thing at the conclusion of trial and find Jasmine Zachary not guilty of all charges brought against her — not because I've asked but because it is warranted by the evidence or the lack thereof. Thank you."

Judge Ralston watched Salty as he positioned himself at the defense table. *No wonder he is feared by his advisories and known for the ferocious defense of his clients. I'm already wondering about the defendant's guilt and haven't even heard the evidence.* Then the judge announced, "I have another matter to attend to so we will break early for lunch and reconvene at 1:30 p.m. sharp to start testimony."

The courtroom rapidly emptied as the gallery was anxious for the lunch break after sitting for what seemed like a long period of time. The bailiff took the jury back to the jury room where lunch was catered.

Jas was escorted back to the holding area and provided lunch which she shoved aside. Her emotions were running wild and her stomach in a knot. She was relieved that at long last the trial was underway as the waiting was torture but, on the other hand, she was scared stiff at what the outcome might be. She was, however, somewhat encouraged after hearing Sam's opening statement. Even knowing she was guilty of the crime, she was able to see the logic the jury could glean from his rendition of what could and in all probability would cause reasonable doubt.

Salty and Buddha, bundled against the wind and snow, hastened across the street to the deli. They ordered sandwiches to go. Salty wanted to review his notes before testimony officially commenced so they took their lunch and retired to an empty interview room at the courthouse.

When Salty was in trial his mind was focused on the task at hand and he engaged in little else to the extent of shutting out even the conversations that went on around him. Buddha knew not to interrupt when Salty was concentrating so he went to the window of the small interview room and watched the snowflakes falling aimlessly to the ground as he munched on his sandwich.

AFTER THE LUNCH break, Judge Ralston took the bench and without further ado rapped his gavel and barked, "Call your first witness, Ms. Cooper."

"The prosecution, as its first witness, calls Dr. Walter Grosso to the stand," Cooper said as she nodded to the bailiff.

The bailiff exited the courtroom and hastened into the corridor. Moments later he led Dr. Walter Grosso into the courtroom. Since there was a sequester order in effect, only the witness who was to testify could be present.

When Jas raised her eyebrows, Buddha whispered, "Judge Ralston doesn't want the witnesses to hear each other's testimony to prevent collusion."

Dr. Walter Grasso entered the courtroom with a swagger which implied a great deal of self-confidence or more appropriately egotism. He walked up to the reporter's table and raised his right hand without being told to do so. Quite obviously he was no stranger to the courtroom and wanted the jury to know it.

Judge Ralston swore in the witness. "Raise your right hand." Grasso did so. "Do you solemnly swear to tell the truth, the whole truth and nothing but the truth so help you God?" Judge Ralston did not agree with the decree to eliminate "God" from the oath and he refused to do so. If the witness didn't believe in God then it was a moot point. However, if the witness was a believer, having to swear to God, according to Judge Ralston's belief, would have some effect on the truthfulness of the testimony about to be rendered. If a witness even thought about challenging the oath, one look at the expression on the judge's face would be dissuasion enough.

"I do," responded Dr. Grasso.

The judge gestured for Dr. Grasso to be seated and, directing his attention at the prosecutor's table, said, "Ms. Cooper..."

"Thank you, Your Honor." Cooper stood and approached the witness, "Doctor, would you please state and spell your full name, your address and occupation for the record?"

The witness straightened and adjusted his suit jacket. He leaned forward and spoke in a clear voice directly into the microphone adjacent to the witness chair, "My name is Walter Paul Grasso, W A L T E R P A U L G R A S S O. I live at 24627 Bernalillo Avenue, Albuquerque, New Mexico. I work for the New Mexico Bureau of Investigation, NMBI, located in Albuquerque. I have been so employed for eighteen years."

"Thank you, Dr. Grasso." Cooper then went to the podium and, examining her notes, asked, "What is your exact field of expertise?"

"I am a forensic pathologist."

"Would you, for the jury, please explain in layman's terms what a forensic pathologist does?"

Dr. Grasso straightened his back and, looking smug, stated, "I examine bodies to determine cause of death."

"Thank you, Doctor. Your Honor, the defense was provided with Dr. Grasso's curriculum vitae through discovery. Does the defense desire us to go through his education, training and experience or will the defense stipulate to Dr. Grasso's qualifications?"

Judge Ralston looked at Salty and asked, "Mr. Morton?"

"In the interest of conserving judicial time, Your Honor, the defense will stipulate to Dr. Grasso's credentials."

"So noted on the record. Ms. Cooper, you may proceed."

"Dr. Grasso, would you please lead us through the autopsy of Nicholas McGregor and explain what your findings revealed?"

It was hard not to notice the witness' arrogant demeanor as he spoke. "I conducted an autopsy on Nicholas McGregor on July 25 at Sacred Heart Hospital here in Farmington. My examination disclosed that Mr. McGregor died of a knife wound to the chest just below the heart. The weapon was a smooth bladed knife, six inches long with a four inch handle. The initial wound was not sufficient enough to instantly kill the victim. He died from bleeding out over a period of time. I would estimate not more than two or three minutes."

"In your opinion, Dr. Grasso, would a woman be able to administer a wound of that nature?"

Grasso was quick to answer. "Oh, yes. The knife penetrated the soft tissue between the ribs just under the heart."

"Thank you, doctor. I have no further questions."

"Mr. Morton, your witness," said Judge Ralston.

Salty stood and asked as he proceeded to the podium, "Dr. Grasso, did you observe any other marks, either fresh or healed, on Mr. McGregor's body?"

"No." Grasso leaned back and crossed his legs. "As far as I could tell, he was in perfect physical condition except, of course, for the knife wound."

"And you state that a woman would be able to administer that serious of a wound. Was the victim stabbed from the front or back?"

"He was stabbed from the front."

"In your opinion, Doctor, would the victim have seen the assault coming? In other words, would the perpetrator have had to thrust the knife forward rather than just slip it into the victim's body?"

"H-m-m-m, I would say a thrust was in order given the excellent physical condition of the victim. His muscle tone would have made it somewhat difficult to just slip the knife in."

"So, being assaulted from the front, the victim most likely saw the blow coming and would probably have fended it off. And if that were the case, wouldn't he have defensive wounds on his body?"

Grasso squinted at Salty, "Well, yes, but this is only speculation."

"My point is, Doctor, a woman the size of my client would find it difficult to subdue the victim while she stabbed him if he was inclined to fend off the assault. He would then most likely have other defensive wounds probably on his hands or arms." Salty leaned forward on the podium, "Would you agree with that?"

Sounding defensive and less confident, Grasso replied, "Yes, I would agree. However, we don't know if the victim saw it coming and would therefore have had time to fend it off. All we know for certain is that he was stabbed from the front and eventually bled out from the wound."

"Thank you, Doctor." Salty returned to the defense table, "I have no further questions Your Honor."

"Ms. Cooper, redirect?"

"No further questions, Your Honor."

"The witness may step down." The judge waited for Dr. Grasso to clear the witness box and exit the courtroom. He then said, "Ms. Cooper, you may call your next witness."

"The prosecutions calls Marcus Salazar as its next witness." Cooper nodded to the bailiff who exited the courtroom and returned with Marcus Salazar.

The witness was sworn in and led through the identification routine by Cooper. Salty once again stipulated to the witness' curriculum vitae.

Cooper began, "Mr. Salazar, what is your field of expertise at the NMBI."

"I'm a fingerprint expert. I compare and analyze fingerprints." Assuming a more comfortable position, Salazar leaned back and crossed his legs.

Cooper continued with the expected line of questioning, "Did you find prints on the murder weapon recovered from Nicholas McGregor's body?"

"Yes. I found only one set of prints on the murder weapon. They matched back to those of the defendant, Jasmine Zachary."

Cooper glanced at the defendant, "Would you be able to tell if any other prints on the knife had been wiped away or smeared prior to Ms. Zachary handling it?"

"No." Salazar furrowed his brow, "There is no way to establish that especially with the amount of blood that had accumulated on the handle of the knife."

"I see. And," Cooper looked toward the jury, "were there other prints collected from the crime scene?"

"Yes, there were many but most of the fingerprints I examined belonged to Nicholas McGregor, Ms. Zachary and an Adell Carlton."

A mummer rippled through the gallery and Judge Ralston banged his gavel restoring order.

"Thank you, Mr. Salazar. The people have no further questions." Cooper took her seat at the prosecution table.

"Your witness," the judge said to Salty.

"Mr. Salazar," Salty began as he rose from his seat, "you stated the only identifiable prints belonged to the victim, Ms. Zachary and Adell Carlton. How many other sets of prints were collected from the scene?"

"Oh, numerous sets. I would say fifteen or so."

Salty moved to the podium, "Did you attempt to match these prints with any you had on file at the NMBI?"

"Yes, we examined every set that we collected." The witness appeared to be insulted at the insinuation that he was derelict in his duties. He snapped, "There were no other matches in our records."

Salty repeated, "No other matches in your records." Then he asked, "What other records are available?"

"Well," Salazar squirmed in his chair, "we don't have the luxury of sending our evidence to DC to be run on the main system containing millions of fingerprints. So, to answer your question, no other records were available to us."

"Mr. Salazar, given the seriousness of the charge, wouldn't you think a complete and thorough examination was warranted?"

"Yes, sir, I do." Salazar lifted his chin in a defiant gesture then said, "However, we only have X-amount of resources and we do the best we can with what we have and what is made available to us."

"I understand. Thank you, Mr. Salazar." Salty turned and said, "Your Honor, I have no further questions."

Cooper was on her feet, "Your Honor, I have redirect for the witness."

"Go ahead, Ms. Cooper."

"Mr. Salazar, were the prints handled in the same way all other prints would be handled?"

Salazar frowned, "Could you repeat the question?"

"Specifically, did you examine the prints collected from the McGregor mansion the same way you would examine any other prints brought to your office for identification?"

"Why, yes." Salazar shot Salty a scathing glance, "I do not cut corners or do sloppy work. I take pride in my work and always endeavor to do the best job I can."

"Thank you. No further questions."

"Mr. Salazar, you may step down."

The last expert witness, Leonard Johnston, was called and asked to give the same identifying information. Upon completion of the routine, Cooper asked, "Mr. Johnston, what is your field of expertise?"

"Chemist. I examine samples of DNA and other bodily fluids as well as any other evidence collected from crime scenes."

"Mr. Johnston, will you describe for the court and jury what evidence you examined that was collected from the McGregor crime scene and what your findings were?"

"Upon examination, the murder weapon revealed that the only blood on the knife belonged to the deceased."

"Is this the same knife you examined for blood samples?" Cooper asked handing a plastic evidence bag containing a knife to the witness.

"Yes, it is." Johnston assumed an air of confidence as he took the bag. "The knife we examined had a notch toward the end of the wooden handle and I can clearly see it there on the handle and I can attest that this is one and the same."

"Thank you." Cooper replaced the knife on the evidence table and said, "Please continue with your testimony as to the rest of the evidence examined from the crime scene."

"There was a multitude of dishes, glasses and utensils collected from the kitchen that I examined. I found an abundant amount of the deceased's DNA as well as that of Ms. Zachary's on these items. I also found a small amount of DNA on a drinking glass corresponding to a saliva samples taken from Adell Carlton."

Salty blinked in disbelief. *Did I hear that right? The prosecution has just established that Carlton had been in the mansion the day of the murder.*

The witness continued, "Other samples were taken but were not identifiable. Items taken from the bathrooms were likewise linked back to the deceased and Ms. Zachary. I also examined the photographs of the tire tracks. They matched Ms. Zachary's car and also a car belonging to Carlton Realty. These tracks were photographed the day of the murder as it had rained and the tracks were still very clear."

"Thank you, Mr. Johnston." Cooper looked at the judge, "I have no further questions."

"Very well, your witness, Mr. Morton," said Judge Ralston.

"Mr. Johnston, you testified you were able to match three samples of DNA to three known persons, Ms. Zachary, the victim and Adell Carlton." Salty rose and walked boldly to the podium. "However, other DNA was tested that you could not match because you had no known source, is that correct?"

"Yes, that is correct."

"And, you stated there were two separate sets of tire tracks photographed the day Mr. McGregor was murdered and law enforcement was able to obtain photographs of the tracks only because it had rained earlier that day. Otherwise, I take it, it would have been impossible to determine how many vehicles may have visited the residence on that particular day. Is that correct?"

"Yes."

"So, to summarize your testimony, Mr. Johnston, what I ascertain is that although you were able to match evidence to known samples you had in hand, there was a plethora of evidence collected that could not be matched. Do you concur with that summary?"

Johnston fidgeted, looking as though he knew what was coming. He responded, "Yes, that sounds about right."

"Then how is it my client, Ms. Zachary, has been singled out as the perpetrator of the crime when it is obvious there were others at the scene who are faceless and nameless? She was found covered with the victim's blood trying to comfort him; she attempted to remove the knife from his chest hoping that would improve his chance of survival; she did not attempt to wipe her prints from the murder weapon; she did not try to cover up any evidence or leave the scene, in fact, she was the one who called 911 and summoned help immediately upon discovering the body. Does that sound like something a murderer would do?"

"OBJECTION!" shouted Cooper, as she erupted from her seat. Johnston, however, had begun to answer: "I'm not qualified to answer that question..."

Judge Ralston somewhat agitated, said: "Mr. Morton, save some of your opinions for your closing argument. Objection sustained. The jury is instructed to disregard the question and answer. The witness is instructed not to respond until I have ruled on an objection."

"Yes, of course, I apologize," Salty said to Judge Ralston and turning back to the witness said, "I was just incensed that the evidence you and the other experts tested was construed to make my client look like the only one who could possibly have committed the murder when there are others who are also likely suspects. My client had no motive to kill Nick McGregor, her only involvement with him was employment. Everything she did upon discovering the body indicates she wanted to save his life, not end it. Is that not true?"

"YOUR HONOR, OBJECTION! The defense is going beyond the scope of direct."

"Objection sustained, Mr. Morton...."

"Yes, Your Honor. I believe I've completed my cross. Thank you, Mr. Johnston."

It was 4:30 p.m. by the time the prosecution's experts finished testifying. Judge Ralston, after instructing the jury not to read, listen to or discuss anything about the case at bar, announced court would adjourn for the day and would reconvene at 9:00 a.m. the following morning.

AND AT 9:00 a.m. sharp the following day, Judge Ralston called the court to order.

Salty respected the way Judge Ralston conducted his courtroom. He was definitely a no-nonsense judge and was earning the respect of everyone in the courtroom.

Jas sat stoic beside Salty at the defense table. He gave her a searching look but was unable to determine what she was thinking. Before he had a chance to speak to her, Cooper was at the podium calling her next witness.

The morning passed slowly as the prosecution parad-
ed law enforcement and emergency team witnesses before
the court. Their testimony was as anticipated. Cooper asked
each as to what they observed upon arrival at the scene. They
testified that the defendant was sitting on the floor in a pud-
dle of blood cradling the victim and sobbing uncontrolla-
bly. Her only statement was that she found him like that and
called 911.

The crime scene investigators testified as to the manner
in which they collected and handled the evidence at the crime
scene and how they transported the evidence to the New Mexico Bureau of Investigation in Albuquerque. They stated they
personally handed each of the experts the sealed bagged evidence and had the experts sign a receipt for the same. This was
the protocol in place to preserve what was called in police par-
lance the chain of custody. There was nothing new or unexpected presented by law enforcement or the EMTs presentation. Their testimony was bland and considered *pro forma*.

Salty cross-examined each witness and, satisfied that they
were all telling the truth, did not try to impeach them.

At the conclusion of the last witness' testimony, Cooper
informed the court that the prosecution's case was complete
and that the people rested. Judge Ralston looked at the clock
mounted over the double doors at the rear of the courtroom.
It was 4:45 p.m. The judge announced they would recess for
the day and commence again at 9:00 a.m. the following morning when the defense would be given the opportunity to present its case.

The jury was escorted out. Jas was returned to jail and
soon the courtroom was empty. Salty and Buddha, upon leaving the courthouse were greeted by ten inches of white fluffy
snow that had fallen during the afternoon court session. As
the two of them parted, they arranged to meet at Salty's office
at 6:00 a.m. the following morning to continue preparing the
defense's case-in-chief. Salty was buoyed by how the day had

gone and waited in excited anticipation for his turn in the barrel. After hearing the experts' testimony, Salty decided to alter his strategy with regard to some of his questions in order to adjust to the tempo established by the prosecution's case-in-chief.

13
FLASH FLOODING

Promptly at 9:00 a.m. the following morning, court reconvened. Judge Ralston, in his morning voice, said, "Mr. Morton, you may call your first witness."

"Thank you, Your Honor. The defense calls Adell Carlton." Salty said, as he pushed his chair back to stand. He felt Jas jerk when he mentioned Carlton's name.

Salty knew Adell would be a hostile witness from Buddha's interview of her. She was just as evasive when he interviewed her. Today, he didn't know exactly what to expect which was a deviation from tradition and a breach of the cardinal rule "Don't ask the question if you don't know the answer." He wrestled with using her. However, in the end, he felt Adell was most likely the murderer and decided to chance it and call her to the stand anyway. He was fairly sure that the benefits of her testimony would outweigh the detriments and might very well be the lynch-pin in the defenses' quest for an acquittal.

The bailiff exited the courtroom and summoned Adell who was waiting in the corridor with Winston and the other sequestered witnesses. Adell and Winston were sitting on one of the wooden benches quietly holding hands waiting in, what appeared to be, nervous anticipation. When Adell's name was called, they both jumped. Adell looked at Winston with a worried expression, squeezed his hand and walked briskly toward the courtroom.

When Adell entered, she tentatively looked around. The gallery was looking back at her. Adell was dressed prim-and-proper in a dark suit. Her white high necked blouse was buttoned to the top. Judge Ralston beckoned her to the front of the courtroom. She quickly walked forward and was sworn in. She, understandably, looked apprehensive as she took the stand and sat in a stilted pose with her hands clasped together in her lap.

Salty let the drama mount as he slowly rose and moved to the podium. He stood there a minute rummaging through his notes. He looked up at Adell and shuffled some more notes.

"Mr. Morton," the judge said in an irritated voice, "we're waiting."

"Of course, Your Honor. Just one moment. I seem to have misplaced something...oh, here it is." Then, directing his gaze at the witness, Salty asked, "Would you please state your full name and spell it for the record?"

"Adell Jean Carlton, A D E L L J E A N C A R L T O N."

"And, Mrs. Carlton, are you employed?"

"Yes. My husband, Winston, and I own our own business."

"And what type business might that be?"

"We own and operate Carlton Realty."

"Is your business located in the city of Farmington?"

"Yes, of course." Salty detected a hint of irritation in Adell's voice.

"Do your day-to-day operations take you beyond Farmington proper?"

"Why, yes." Adell crossed her arms over her chest.

This is turning into a real challenge. She's having trouble disguising dislike for me. "Where else do you have listings?" Salty asked.

Adell answered in short clipped sentences, "We do most of our showings in town. We also operate throughout all of San Juan County. We are licensed to sell anywhere in New Mexico."

"Are you familiar with The Desert Rose Estates?"

"Most certainly." Her voice was as strained as a taut wire. *She's afraid of something.* "Do you list property in that area?"

"Of course. That was and is a major project. The contractors have expanded and are still building there. There are some stately old mansions peppered in with the new construction. It has become somewhat of a showplace and the old and new complement each other creating a charming atmosphere conducive to successful sales." Adell answered the question, sounding every bit like a real estate agent talking to a client.

"Do you spend much time in that area?"

"I don't know what much time means. Would you clarify?"

"Are you there quite often in the early afternoons on week days?"

Adell barked, "Quite often? No!"

"Let me remind you that you're under oath. Do you understand the consequences of perjury? You could be charged and convicted of a felony which would mean forfeiting your real estate license. Now, with that in mind, do you desire to change your answer to the last question?"

Adell fidgeted in her chair, crossed and uncrossed her legs, seemingly unable to find a comfortable position for her arms and finally said in a softer tone, "Yes, I would like to restate my last answer. I do visit The Desert Rose Estates regularly and frequently visited an old friend who once lived there."

Salty breathed a sigh of relief, "And, what is your old friend's name?"

Adell, looked as though she knew there was no escape. She said in a resigned voice, "Nick McGregor."

The courtroom became hushed. You could hear a pin drop. It seemed the gallery was holding its collective breath for more than a healthy length of time.

"Mrs. Carlton," Salty continued, "would you say perhaps every weekday you paid Mr. McGregor a visit?"

"Maybe. I don't know if it was *EVERY* weekday but quite often nonetheless."

"What were you doing at McGregor's house every day?"

After a long pause, Adell muttered what sounded like, "I refuse to answer that question!"

At least, Judge Ralston interpreted it that way. In a stern voice, he demanded, "Mrs. Carlton, you cannot withhold pertinent information concerning this case! I'm ordering you to answer the question!"

"NO! I will not answer the question." Adell said defiantly.

It was obvious to Salty that the judge was losing his patience. "I will give you one more chance to answer. Otherwise, I am going to hold you in contempt of court." He then demanded, "Mrs. Carlton, answer the question!"

Adell just sat there and glared at the judge. After a long pause, Judge Ralston ordered, "Guard, take Mrs. Carlton into custody." And, looking at Adell, the judge said with controlled anger, "I'm holding you in contempt of court."

A DEPUTY SHERIFF came forward. He handcuffed and escorted Adell out the side door of the courtroom. Winston, waiting for his turn to testify, was in a position to observe that Adell was handcuffed and had been placed in custody. His first thought was that she had been arrested for Nick McGregor's murder. It was then he decided to throw himself on his sword.

Judge Ralston finally restored order and then declared a ten-minute recess. He commanded the attorneys to join him in his chambers.

Salty was almost alarmed at the anger the judge spewed at him. "Morton, I'm giving you fair warning, you will not turn my courtroom into a circus. Do you have any more theatrics up your sleeve?"

"Your Honor, I did not plan or even imagine my witness would react in such a fashion. In fact, she was in essence not my witness but a 'hostile witness.' My next witness is her husband, Winston Carlton, a hostile witness as well, and I cannot guarantee he will not react much the same way."

The judge rubbed his face with his hands and grunted but knew he was unable to do anything about the situation. He had never been overturned on appeal and did not intend to start this late in his career. He understood only too well the uncertainties of trial and the precarious nature of hostile witnesses.

When court reconvened, Salty asked the bailiff to call Winston Carlton.

Winston, encouraged by his determination, walked briskly to the front of the courtroom, was sworn in and took the witness chair. Attempting to disguise his hate, Winston just glared at Salty.

"Would you please state and spell your name for the record?" Salty began.

His voice was laced with anxiety as he answered, "My name is Winston Carlton, W I N S T O N C A R L T O N." Then he paused for a brief instant before stating, "I want to confess to murdering Nick McGregor."

The courtroom erupted into a wild frenzy. Reporters scrambled and ran over the top of each other in their quest to be the first to report the breaking news. Judge Ralston pounded his gavel with so much force that it broke under the strain. Buddha put his arm around Jas as she swooned and became faint. Salty stood paralyzed, unable to fathom what he had just heard. To say chaos ruled supreme would be an understatement.

When the judge finally restored order and, masking his anger fairly well, he asked Salty to continue in his examination of Winston Carlton.

Not wanting this opportunity to slip through his fingers, Salty said, "Mr. Carlton, would you please inform the jury as to how you perpetrated the murder?"

Winston slumped in the witness chair as he replied, "I will not make a statement other than I killed Nick McGregor. That's all I'm going to say."

Salty, still recovering from the shock, looked at the judge and shrugged his shoulders. Then before the judge could speak, Salty moved to dismiss the case against Jas on the grounds that Winston's confession to having murdered Nick McGregor was tantamount to an exoneration of his client.

The judge looked at Cooper with raised eyebrows. "Well...," he said.

Cooper asked the Court if she could briefly examine the witness and was granted the request.

"Mr. Carlton, when you admitted to killing Nick McGregor, did you realize that this was a capital offense punishable by life in prison? Knowing this, do you still persist in your claim that you perpetrated the murder?"

"Yes, I do understand the consequences of my actions. I don't want an innocent person like Ms. Zachary to be punished for something I did."

Cooper sat in stunned silence apparently not knowing what to say.

Salty, still standing at the podium, said, "Your Honor, may I ask the witness another question?"

Judge Ralston, still shaking his head, replied, "Proceed."

"Mr. Carlton, was Jasmine Zachary, the defendant in this case, in any way involved in Nick McGregor's death?"

"Absolutely not!" was the firm response from Winston as he stared at Salty without remorse.

Never having been faced with such a dilemma, Judge Ralston recessed court until the following day. To the jurors, he again reiterated his previous dictate only this time with more authority. "Do not, and I repeat, do not listen to, read or watch anything that might appear on television or in any other news source concerning this trial. Do not talk about the case among yourselves. You will report back here promptly at 9:00 a.m. tomorrow morning." Then he ordered the attorneys to meet with him in chambers.

The courtroom was cleared. Jas, having been revived, was returned to her cell. Winston was taken into temporary custody to be interrogated by law enforcement concerning his confession. The attorneys left to meet with the judge in his chambers. Buddha stood and headed for the door extracting his cellphone from his pocket. He wanted to call Jordan as soon as he could. *I thought those Perry Mason trials were somewhat far-fetched when a witness confessed to the crime on the stand. Guess Salty one-upped Perry.*

SITTING ON HER cold hard bunk, alone in her cell, Jas wallowed in confusion.

Jas' head was spinning. *What on Earth just happened? Why in the world would Winston Carlton confess to something I did? I just... I just don't understand what's going on. Surely this isn't God's doing. If it is, I don't deserve it. Is this all still part of the nightmare?*

14
CLEAR SKIES

Judge Ralston hung his robe on the coatrack in his office and took a seat behind his modest desk in a not so modest leather swivel chair. He was beginning to look haggard. He laced his fingers together on the desk in front of him and said, "Where do we go from here?"

Salty, having had a few minutes to compose his thoughts, decided he would ask for dismissal with prejudice which would prohibit Jas from ever being retried for the murder of Nick McGregor under any circumstances.

Looking at Cooper, Salty said, "I'm going to file a motion to dismiss with prejudice."

Cooper began to shake her head, "I don't know," she said, "The evidence certainly points to your client as the perp."

"And how does that trump an outright confession?" Salty retorted. "It's obvious to everyone but you that you're prosecuting an innocent person."

"You have a point. However, in the interest of justice, the People will concur with the defense's proposal and dismiss the case, only *without* prejudice."

"Un-huh! No dice. Dismissal *with* prejudice or we finish the trial."

"Ms. Cooper," Judge Ralston interjected, "do you see any other outcome if the case is decided by the jury? They heard Carlton confess on the stand. My feeling is if you pursue this case to the end you will certainly alienate the jury and may I remind you this is a jury that has already sat through over two weeks of trial. Besides, a conviction under the circumstances would be a recipe for reversal. Do you really think the jury will now return a guilty verdict?"

"You also make a good point, Judge. I really do not see any other alternative. If the jury returns a not guilty verdict that would be the same as dismissal with prejudice. So, in order to conserve judicial time and spare the defendant more anxiety than necessary, since it appears she did not commit the murder, I will not oppose the defense's request."

"Fine!" The judge reared back in his chair, "Mr. Morton, prepare the appropriate motion and proposed order and have them ready when we reconvene tomorrow morning? Needless to say, I will be granting the motion."

"Your Honor, it would be my pleasure indeed. Thank you both. If there's nothing else, I would like confer with my client and relate the good news."

"Yes, of course. I have nothing else. Ms. Cooper?"

"No, Your Honor. The prosecution has nothing further."

JAS SAT NERVOUSLY twisting a tissue. When she heard the outer door of the pod open she jumped to her feet. Moments later Salty was being ushered into her cell. She threw her arms around his neck and hugged him. He gently pushed her back and looked into, what he perceived, her innocent big blue eyes. "I have some good, no, great news," he began. "The court will be dismissing your case with prejudice when we reconvene tomorrow morning."

The case is going to be dismissed and WITH PREJUDICE. Can it be?

Jas knew from her brief summer job working for lawyers that *with prejudice* meant she could never be retried for the same crime. If it was dismissed without prejudice and more evidence or other circumstances surfaced, she could be brought back and retried. In legal terms, once the case was dismissed *with* prejudice or the jury found the defendant not guilty, jeopardy attached and to bring the defendant back before the court on the same charge would be considered *double jeopardy* and not constitutionally permitted.

Oh, please God, don't let anything happen between now and tomorrow to unravel the dismissal agreement. I really didn't mean to kill Nick and I'm ever so sorry. I miss him so much I can hardly bear it. Please forgive me. I don't understand why Winston confessed but I'm sure a case cannot be proven against him anyway.

ALTHOUGH THE SKIES were cloudy and gray and snow loomed in the forecast, the defense team was elated when they returned to court the following morning. Jordan accompanied Salty and Buddha as this was a red-letter day. Jordan sat in the gallery directly behind the defense table. When all parties were present and the courtroom was filled to capacity, the judge entered and beckoned to the bailiff to call the court to order. Without ceremony, Judge Ralston thereupon asked Salty if he had a motion to present.

"Yes, Your Honor, I have a Motion to Dismiss With Prejudice and a proposed Order to present to the court."

"Ms. Cooper, do you have any objection to the granting of said motion?" Judge Ralston asked.

"No, Your Honor, the People concede and offer no objection."

Once again the courtroom became chaotic. Judge Ralston broke another gavel in a futile attempt to restore order.

Once order was restored, Salty asked to approach the bench and was granted permission. He presented the Motion to Dismiss and Judge Ralston signed the Order granting the same with a flourish. The prosecution had previously been given a copy of the motion for their approval and it bore Cooper's signature. After signing the order, the judge gave the bailiff the signed original to make copies for all parties.

"This case is hereby dismissed *with prejudice*," Judge Ralston announced in a subdued tone. "Ms. Zachary, this means you are free to go." Since his gavel was broken, he just rose and gingerly left the courtroom which was still buzzing with the excitement over the revelation of the dismissal. Only now, the dismissal was official and Jas was free.

The bailiff reappeared and distributed conformed copies of the signed order to each of the attorneys. Jas lovingly fingered Salty's copy. She looked up at him with tears in her eyes. He took her in his arms and they hugged each other, lingering longer than necessary conveying even to the uninitiated more than just gratitude. After embracing Jas, Salty and Cooper met mid-way between their respective tables and shook hands in a gesture of mutual respect. Cooper had her briefcase packed and, as she headed toward the door, she turned and said to Salty, "If I ever get in trouble, you're the man! How'd you pull that off?" They both knew she was kidding—sort of.

SALTY WAITED AT the counter at the detention center while the release papers were being prepared. Jas was ushered into the interior where she retrieved her personal belongings which had been confiscated at the time of her booking. The evidence custodian handed Jas a manila envelope, still sealed, and Jas signed for it. With shaky hands she opened it, peered inside and was relieved to see that the ring was still there. She then joined Salty in the lobby.

"Is it over? Am I really free?" she asked.

Salty tucked her arm under his and urged her toward the exit. He noticed she appeared to be weak and he supported her as they walked to his car. "Yes, my dear. You're really free."

The defense team had prearranged to meet at Salty's office after the release was final. Jordan had purchased a bottle of champagne to celebrate and when the team had assembled, the champagne was uncorked and passed around. The four of them raised their glasses high in grateful homage to the powers that be. After they had exhausted the bottle, Salty invited all to lunch and the celebration continued into the late afternoon.

As the party finally waned, Jas said, "I haven't been home in five months, Salty, I'm homesick."

"Of course you are. How insensitive of me." After Salty paid the check, he stood signaling the party was over. He held Jas' chair for her and said to Jordan and Buddha, "See you two back at the office," and escorted Jas to the door.

Jas had confided in Salty that she had some money saved and when she was incarcerated she gave it to Yvonne. Yvonne used the savings to keep Jas' utilities and other payments current at both her home and boutique.

Although she was exonerated, Jas was concerned that her infamy would keep potential customers from engaging her services as an interior designer. While still in jail, she was contacted by a free-lance writer who asked if she would let him do a story on her. She said she would think about it and contact him later. Instead, she decided she would attempt to write a book and tell the story in her own words. She had been a journalism major in college and the prospect of writing an autobiography excited her. She could publish it as fiction and embellish it a bit. Looking on the bright side, if her business waned, she would have plenty of time to write.

WINSTON CARLTON WAS taken into custody but he was not booked immediately. Law enforcement wanted to interrogate him before charges were filed. Consequently, Winston spent the night in jail. Late the next morning, he was led into a brightly lit interrogation room where he sat and waited for what seemed like an eternity. The steel table had eyelets riveted to the top for handcuffing hostile detainees. The drab light green paint on the walls was peeling. The floor was dirty and the room smelled like stale liquor. Winston suddenly felt nauseous. The emotional trauma of having confessed to a crime he didn't commit and his present surroundings made his stomach churn. He hoped he wouldn't vomit; that would show weakness and that was something he could and would not tolerate. Winston was sick with apprehension not knowing what was happening with Adell. *Had they released her as a result of my confession or was she sitting in a room just like this one? Did she know I confessed? Dammit! Why won't anyone tell me anything?*

Two detectives finally came in. They were chatting about the outcome of Jas' trial in general and the previous day's events in particular.

Winston asked them what all the excitement was about.

They looked at Winston with steely eyes.

"It's not an everyday occurrence that murder charges against a defendant are dismissed in the middle of trial based on the confession of another purported perpetrator. That would be you!" Sgt. Bridges sneered. "The chief wants us to interview you regarding how and why you killed McGregor."

Winston said caustically, "I'm not making any statement until you tell me what has become of my wife, Adell Carlton."

The detectives looked at each other in amazement. "You mean the woman they arrested for contempt of court for refusing to answer a question?"

"WHAT?" Winston sprang from the chair and leaned his hands on the table top to steady himself. "What are you saying? You mean she wasn't charged with the murder; that she was taken into custody only for contempt of court at not having answered a question?"

Bridges had taken the chair across from Winston and when Winston jumped up, Bridges demanded, "Hey, sit yourself back down! We're not through here." Then noticing the horror-stricken look on Winston's face, he added, "What! Did you think she also confessed to the murder? Man, it's either feast or famine around here."

Winston looked as though he might faint. "Please! Tell me what happened in there," he begged.

Bridges pointed to Winston's chair. Winston sat back down. "Well, it appears like she refused to answer a question while on the witness stand and the judge ordered her to be jailed. He didn't say for how long. All we know is that there is a hold on her."

"Oh, my God!" Winston cried. "Oh, my God."

"Now what?" Bridges demanded.

"I want to recant my confession."

"You're kidding, of course, aren't you?" Bridges said squinting at Winston.

"NO! I did not kill McGregor. I'm now denying any involvement."

Bridges slapped his thighs with his palms exhibiting disgust, and standing up he said, "Geeze Louise. Lance, get the captain."

Detective Lance Young left the room and Detective Larry Bridges began rummaging through his pockets trying to find his antacid tablets. Within a matter of minutes Detective Young returned with a stern looking man that Winston assumed was the captain.

"Hi, Winston, I'm Captain Logan. I understand you want to withdraw your confession and are now saying you didn't murder Nick McGregor. Is that correct?"

"Damn right. I didn't kill the bastard. How do I right the record?"

"Then why did you confess?" Logan asked and arched his eyebrows.

"That's my business," Winston said with malice in his voice.

Logan, with a frown, asked, "Do you want a lawyer?"

"Only if I need one. How do I prove I didn't do it?"

"A lie detector test would be a good first step."

"All right then, let's do it."

"It's not that easy. We have to set it up and get a techni-
cian. We only have two officers who are trained and experienced polygraphers; one is on sick leave having broken his leg
skiing up at Purgatory last week. The other has been working
his normal duty rotation on the swing shift and he will not be
available until shift change this afternoon at 1500. I'll ask you
again, do you want to call a lawyer?"

"Hell, yes, since I have to spend most of the day in this
godforsaken place, I'm left with no choice."

Logan looked at Bridges who then passed the telephone to
Winston and all three law enforcement officers left the room.

Winston then called Andrew Sinclair, the attorney the
Carlton s had on retainer for their business. They often needed
legal advice during real estate transactions.

"ANDY!" Winston shouted into the phone. "I'm in the
slammer and need your help, pronto."

"Winston," Sinclair replied, "This sounds like a criminal
matter. I'm not a criminal lawyer. My expertise, as you know,
is civil. I don't know how much help I would be to you."

"Damn the torpedoes, Andy. Get your ass over here as
soon as you can or I'm going to replace you as our attorney."

"Calm down, Winston. I'll be there, I'm just saying…"

"Never mind what you're just saying, just get over here.
Bring the checkbook. You need to bail both Adell and me out
of this place." Winston slammed down the receiver not waiting for a reply.

Winston spent a fitful morning in jail. His cell was cold
and the cot was miserably hard. He restlessly paced his cell
waiting for something to happen. He lost track of time and was
surprised it was noon when he was brought lunch. Winston
was much too distraught to eat so he pushed the tray aside and
began pacing again. After another eternity of waiting, Sinclair
was admitted into Winston's cell.

"It's about damn time!" Winston barked.

"Hold on, Winston," Sinclair snapped, "I arrived at noon. I've been waiting for over an hour. They refused to let me in until after lunch was cleared."

"Oh, sorry, Andy. I... I..." Winston was at a loss for words. Apologizing wasn't something he did on a regular basis except maybe to Adell.

Sinclair sat down beside him on the cot and said, "I was told that you requested a polygraph. Have they given you an indication when that would take place?"

"No, they've given me nothing. Can you find out what's going on and especially what has become of Adell," Winston asked with panic in his voice.

"Yes, I did inquire about Adell..."

"Dammit, why didn't you tell me that sooner?" Winston shouted.

"For God's sake, man, I just got here. Keep this up and I'm leaving."

"I'm sorry." Winston cringed. Those words didn't come easily but he didn't want Sinclair to leave. "I'm so distressed that I don't know what I'm doing or saying."

"To answer your question, Judge Ralston will have to decide what to do with her."

"How soon? Any idea?"

"No, it's just wait and see."

"Dammit, I'm tired of waiting. What happens when I pass the polygraph? Will they let me go?"

Sinclair stood before answering, "I can't say at this point. It all depends on what other evidence they have against you. Do you know of anything other than your confession?"

"Hell's fire and damnation, Andy, I was never in that house so they couldn't have much." Winston laid back on the cot and put his arm over his forehead.

Sinclair, leaning against the bars, finally asked, "What in God's name made you confess in the first place?"

Winston groaned, "I knew Adell was seeing McGregor. When I saw them take her out in cuffs, I thought she was being arrested for the murder. In order to save her, I decided to confess."

"Did you explain this to the detectives?"

"No. When I requested an attorney, they quit questioning me."

Sinclair nodded and said, "I'm going to leave now and find out what's going on. You try to calm down. If you're emotionally upset it may have a bearing on the poly. I'll be back as soon as I know something. Okay?"

Winston sat up, "Okay, Andy. Thanks."

SINCLAIR WENT TO the main desk and asked to speak to the officer in charge. Sergeant Preston was called to the counter. He introduced himself and asked Sinclair what he could do for him.

"Good afternoon, Sergeant. I'm Andy Sinclair and I represent the Carltons. I understand Mr. Carlton is scheduled for a polygraph, presumably today. Can you tell me at what time that has been scheduled for?"

"Looks like, h-m-m-m, just about now," Preston said examining his clipboard. "Do you want to be present for the examination?"

"Of course. Where will it be conducted?"

"We have our own facility right here in the detention center." Preston looked past Sinclair and stated, "Look, they're bringing your client in now. I'll grease the skids for you so you won't have any problem watching from a connecting room that has a two-way mirror."

"Thank you. Where shall I wait?"

"Just stay here, I'll be right back."

Sinclair was granted permission to confer with Winston before the polygraph commenced. After Winston was advised of the protocol, he was ushered into the polygraph room where the police polygrapher administered the test which took less than an hour.

While they awaited the test results, Sinclair was asked to remain in a waiting room and Winston was returned to his cell. Approximately forty-five minutes later, Sinclair was advised of the results.

DETECTIVES BRIDGES AND Young arrived back at the station house early enough to be present when the results of Winston's polygraph examination were posted.

"I knew it! Damn the luck, I just knew it!" Bridges raved and waved his arms wildly around in frustration. He stormed into his office and called Cooper to pass on the results of the polygraph hoping it wasn't too late for something to be salvaged out of the whole sorry mess.

Bridges was informed Cooper had not yet arrived back at the office from Farmington. Bridges flushed with frustration. He left word for her to call him IMMEDIATELY upon her return. He knew Cooper didn't carry a cell phone. She confided in him that she would often forget to turn it off in court and was admonished on more than one occasion by the presiding judge so she opted not to carry one at all. It was too humiliating to be dressed down in court in front of God and everyone.

Bridges constantly checked his watch as time crawled by. He paced up and down waiting for the call. He telephoned twice more just to make sure Cooper received his message. Finally he got the return call.

"What's up?" Cooper demanded.

"Hold on to your hat, counselor. Carlton recanted his confession when he learned his wife was only being held on contempt charges. He asked for and took a poly. The sorry sucker thought Adell was being arrested for the murder and he was playing the martyr in order to save her. He passed the poly and we, of course, other than his now withdrawn confession, don't have a shred of evidence to link him to the murder.

The local DA's office authorized his release since there is nothing to hold him on." Bridges paused and then asked, "Where do we go from here?"

"Good question. Where can we go from here?" The silence lasted a few seconds, then Cooper added, "The case has been dismissed, and with prejudice I might add. We have no recourse. I hate like hell for her to get away with it but..."

"Me too. I'm numb." Bridges paused, then said, "I'm going home and drain a gallon of gin and sleep for a week. Thanks for the valiant effort. Take it easy, counselor." He replaced the phone in its cradle and headed out the door for home. As she hung up the phone, Cooper was wondering if maybe she could also use a drink or two.

15
HURRICANE WARNINGS

C ongratulations," said Sinclair when he entered Winston's cell. "You passed with flying colors and, just as you surmised, the DA has no evidence that you were in or upon the McGregor premises at any time whatsoever. The lab compared your prints and DNA that you provided upon your admittance with samples collected from the crime scene and nothing matched back to you."

"HA! I told you so!" Winston plopped down on the cot, relief written on his face. He then demanded, "How soon can I see Adell?"

Sinclair put one foot on the cot and, with his forearm resting on his thigh, he leaned toward Winston. "Judge Ralston took pity and sentenced Adell to time served and she is free to leave."

"That is wonderful news. Thanks, Andy."

"Just doing my job." Sinclair said as he picked at a speck of lint on his trousers. "After I explained why you confessed, the DA decided not to pursue charges against you. They could have nailed your ass with false reporting but in light of what a cluster this whole ordeal has turned into they opted not to take any further action."

JUDITH BLEVINS

Winston, with a faraway look in his eyes, said, "So the murder of Nick McGregor still remains a mystery?"

"So it appears. Not our worry. Let's get you processed and out of here."

Winston stood. "Damn straight! I'm ready, Andy. Where's Adell now?"

"She's being processed as we speak and we'll meet her in the front lobby."

When Adell saw Winston, she rushed into his open arms and embraced him with all her might. Babbling through a torrent of tears, she said, "Oh, my Darling, you were willing to sacrifice yourself to save me. I should be angry with you for thinking I did it, but I'm not." She pushed Winston back and stared straight into his teary eyes, "I understand why you would think I did it, but I just want you to know that Nick and I were never romantically involved. We were just platonic friends. That's all!"

"Then, why all the secrecy?" Winston murmured.

Twisting a tissue, Adell said, "I was helping him study for his realtor license. I didn't mention it in court when they started badgering me because, even to me, it sounded like a lame excuse and besides Nick asked me to keep it a secret."

Adell turning away and then back again, continued, "He didn't want it known that he was having financial difficulties and was forced to do something to generate income. He said he started a remodel which turned out to be more expensive than he ever dreamed it would be. In addition, one of his daughters had to have surgery. Her husband was a victim of the failed economy and was out of work and they were not insured. Nick paid the doctor and hospital somewhere in the neighborhood of $195,000.

"I promised not say anything about him obtaining a realty license and his financial woes. I felt I had to honor that promise, and especially now that he's deceased."

Winston nodded but said nothing.

"I had no idea I could really be put in jail for refusing to answer a question and then after it went on so long, that stubborn streak in me wouldn't let me answer and this was the result. I want you to believe that I am guilty only of stupidity. I know I've not been a good wife but, if you'll give me a chance, I'll make it up to you for the rest of our lives. I do love you, Winston."

Winston pulled her into a hug, "Adell, I've never loved anyone else and could never go on without you. And, I'll hold you to that promise."

Sinclair, brushing tears from his eyes, signed the release forms and silently exited the building to where his car was parked. *Thank God I'm a civil lawyer. This crap has been enough to last me the rest of my career. I feel for the criminal defense lawyers who do this day in and day out. No wonder they're a strange breed!*

DOUGLAS "DOUG" GOLDMAN II owned and operated *Goldman's Fine Jewelry* located on the main drag in Farmington. The business had been handed down from his grandfather, who had immigrated to America at the onset of World War II, to his father and now to him. Doug had an only son who he hoped someday would carry on the family tradition. Time would tell as his son had his heart set on becoming a rock star.

Doug Goldman and Detective Larry Bridges were high school buddies. They had participated in sports together and had formed a bond that had endured the test of time. As close friends often do, they met at least once a month for a beer, sports, political commentary and sometimes poker.

Larry entered *Benjie's,* an old but well-kept establishment, and spotted Doug sitting at the bar nursing a beer." Larry crept up behind Doug and slapping him on the back harder than intended said, "Hey, you son-of-a-gun, how's life treating you?"

Jumping slightly and sloshing beer onto the bar, Doug responded, "Pretty good until you interrupted my musings and spilled my brewski."

"You big cry baby. Guess I'll just have to buy you another."

"Yeah. Wish I'd known the 'cry baby' card worked so well. I could be enjoying free beer lo these many years. Damn!"

Larry slid onto the stool next to Doug and ordered two beers, one for him and a replacement for Doug. Sitting there, Larry tossed a handful of peanuts into his mouth and picked up the latest edition of the Farmington Post which someone had carelessly tossed on the bar. The headlines read: *"First Degree Murder Dismissed Against Zachary."*

Doug, glancing at the paper, commented, "Can't you cops ever get it right? Wasn't that the case you were working on?"

"Same one," Larry responded. "It wasn't my idea to drop the charges. Jas danced her way out of that one!"

Doug put his beer down and looked at Larry quizzically.

Larry took a long pull from his bottle then feeling self-conscious, asked, "Why you looking at me like that? Do I have spinach in my teeth?"

"That name, Jas, rings a bell. That's an unusual name and one not easily forgotten."

"Yeah, so…" Larry shoved the paper aside and turned to face his friend.

Doug rubbed his head and frowned. Suddenly Larry noticed Doug's expression change as the "lights" went on. "I just realized," Doug declared, "I engraved a ring for the murdered guy, Nick McGregor. It was a very expensive wide gold band showcasing a two caret near perfect diamond."

Larry's voice rang with excitement as he said, "Yeah, go on…"

"Well, McGregor told me it had belonged to his mother and it was his mother's twenty-fifth anniversary present from his father. McGregor also told me that he and his hopefully soon-to-be fiancé were celebrating one-year of being together the following July and he was going to surprise her with the ring and a proposal. McGregor said he thought the ring inscription would personalize the ring and thus make it *hers* since it had previously belonged to his mother."

Larry rubbed his hands together in exasperation, "Go on Doug, dammit man, get to it!"

"Okay, I'm getting there. Just back off, will ya? The reason I remember is that he had it inscribed '*Jas, Luv U 4-Ever, Nick.*' Jas, as I said, is a very uncommon name. In fact, I'd never heard it before. When you called the defendant Jas it triggered my memory of the inscription."

Larry, absorbed this revelation in the middle of taking a swig of his beer. Finally realizing the significance he choked, coughed and spewed beer out of his mouth and nostrils.

"Son-of-a-bitch! Son-of-a-bitch! Damn it anyway! Would you repeat that? No, never mind, I heard you the first time. Son-of-a-bitch! You still have a record of the engrave?"

Just then the bartender reappeared for the second time in less than ten minutes to wipe up beer spilled by the two. He rolled his eyes in disgust.

"Of course, I keep impeccable records...." Doug answered and wondered if Larry was going to beat his head against the bar as he was in such a frantic state.

"Okay, I need the original receipt. Can you do that for me?"

"Absolutely, but what...."

Doug, looking at Larry, sat there patiently waiting for the explanation he felt certain would be forthcoming. Instead, Larry fumbled for his cellphone and called headquarters.

"Captain, this is Bridges. I just stumbled upon some information that could possibly allow us to reopen the Zachary case."

"What are you talking about?"

"A friend of mine engraved a ring for McGregor implicating him and Jas in an affair. Bingo, there's our motive, jealously! I need a warrant to search Zachary's place."

"I'm on it. I'll have it ready for you in less than an hour. Swing by the station; I want to be in on this!"

"It'll be a few. I'm on my way now to get the engrave receipt."

"I'll be ready."

Upon completion of the call, Larry jumped up and asked Doug if he would take him to his store so he could retrieve the engraving receipt.

"Sure, but…"

"Never mind. I'll explain later."

Larry tossed a twenty dollar bill onto the bar and the two men hastily left. Larry followed Doug to the jewelry store in his car. It took only minutes for Doug to find the receipt. He did keep impeccable records. Once Larry had the receipt in hand, he thanked Doug and rushed out leaving a dazed Doug in the wake.

CAPTAIN LOGAN DIDN'T have to search far for a judge as County Court Judge James Hunter, having worked late, was just leaving the courthouse in his polished black Mercedes when Logan drove up. Logan flagged the judge down and approached the judge's driver's side, badge in hand in case the judge didn't recognize him. Logan explained the situation and asked Judge Hunter to read the affidavit and sign the search warrant. Illuminated by the dome light in his Mercedes, the judge read the affidavit and subsequently signed the warrant. He sealed it with a duplicate official state seal he kept in the glove compartment of his vehicle.

"Thank you, Your Honor," Logan said as he gathered up all three signed and sealed copies.

"Good luck, Son," Judge Hunter replied as he drove off heading for the sanctity of his home and the delicious dinner he knew would be waiting. Judge Hunter did enjoy his wife's cooking and his ample stature was a testimonial to what a good cook she was.

Detective Bridges arrived at police headquarters just as Captain Logan returned from the courthouse.

"We got it!" Captain Logan said and waved the search warrant in the air.

"YES!" Larry high-fived Logan and said, "Come on. Let's get some guys and roll."

On their way to the parking garage, Captain Logan enlisted three street cops to join them in the search. As they raced across town, Logan congratulated Larry on his astute work.

"Damn, Larry, you lucky jerk, this establishes the missing link, the motive for Zachary to have killed McGregor. She declared all along they were not in an intimate relationship. Then out of the blue a ring inscribed with his love and devotion for her falls into your lap. My best guess is, knowing what I know about McGregor, he was diddling the Carlton woman, God knows why. Yuck! Obviously, Zachary found out about it, or at least suspected it. The green-eyed monster then took over and bye-bye Nicky."

"Yeah, that's my take on it as well. Now if we can just find the ring and/or any other evidence proving they were screwing around we may have another shot at it. I'm not sure how *newly found evidence* plays into resurrecting the case in light of that dismissal. That's the DA's bailiwick but we'll do our job and let the chips fall where they may."

"Right on, Bro. Ain't that little lady gonna be surprised! Here she thought she had a get outta jail free card."

JAS WAS ABRUPTLY awakened by a cracking noise at the front door as the lock was jimmied by the search team. *Oh my God, now what.* Jas slipped on her robe and padded barefoot to the door. She was almost run down as a swarm of blues exploded into her foyer.

"Hey! You can't...What's going on..."

Larry cut her off in midsentence, "We have a warrant to search your premises and vehicle, Ms. Zachary, here's your copy. Just step aside and stay outta the way so we can conduct our search? Thank you."

A confused Jas stepped aside. She looked at the warrant in utter disbelief and retreated into the dining room area and quietly sat at the table keeping a watchful eye on the invaders while one of them kept a watchful eye on her.

The officers scattered each taking a separate section of the condominium. Larry found his way to the master bedroom and looked around for a jewelry box or armoire. He found both inside the walk-in closet. The armoire had a hidden drawer, which was a joke. Even the greenest amateur could have ferreted it out. Inside all cozy and snug in a dark blue velvet ring roll was the sought-after prize. Larry recognized it immediately from Doug's description.

"Well, well, well" he thought as he turned it over in his hand reading the inscription: "*Jas, Luv U 4-Ever, Nick.*"

Captain Logan was searching other areas of the master suite when Larry beckoned him over with a jerk of his head. He held the ring up and pointed to the inscription. Logan gave Larry a knowing smile. He had also found an incriminating piece of evidence, Jas' photo album containing up-close and personal pictures of the couple taken during their relationship.

Larry hissed, "How sweet it is!" when Logan showed him the album. He then bagged and labeled his treasure trove.

After the search was concluded, Larry told Jas to get dressed and she was once again placed in custody and transported to police headquarters. She was isolated in the same interrogation room she had occupied many months before. The only thing she said was "I demand my right to call my attorney." The detectives knowing they could not deny this request handed her the phone and hastily left the room.

"Sam, I've been arrested again. Will you please come, I need your help. I'll explain when you get here."

Salty arrived at the police station in less than an hour. When he asked the officers what Jas was being held for he was informed they had *newly discovered evidence* and would be requesting the DA to re-file the first degree murder prosecution against Jas.

"What? That's ridiculous! The case was dismissed *with prejudice* and jeopardy has attached. Even if she confessed you couldn't bring her to trial again."

"That's the DA's call. We're in the process now of informing Ms. Cooper of what has come to light. A copy of the warrant and inventory is being faxed to Albuquerque."

"May I be so bold as to also ask to have a copy of the warrant and inventory?"

Detective Bridges gave Salty a copy of the search warrant including the affidavit therefor and the inventory of items taken into evidence, the fruits of the search so to speak. The first item was, of course, the ring. Salty read and re-read the listed inscription. He shook his head and read it again. He didn't want to believe what he was seeing because he, too, instantly connected the dots. He sat down heavily in one of the visitor's chairs staring out into space completely flabbergasted by this new revelation. After the shock diminished, Salty asked to see his client. He was led into the interrogation room. Jas was seated at the table with her head buried in her folded arms.

JAS LOOKED UP when Salty entered. Her first inclination was to run to him but she quickly discarded that notion when she saw the look of disgust and disappointment on his face.

When Salty put his finger to his lips, Jas knew it was a signal not to blurt out anything. Jas nodded understanding and remained silent. Salty said that he would visit her in jail early the next day. With that he left and Jas was left alone

wallowing in oceans of reflection and desertion. Sam was stoic and she could only imagine what he must be thinking and
feeling. Tomorrow was light years away and way too far out
of reach.

Jas had invoked her right to an attorney and the detectives
knew it was useless and indeed a violation of the law to attempt
to interrogate her. So, they left the jail crew to process her into
custody. The same routine was conducted as before. A mug shot
was taken, she was fingerprinted, her personal items were confiscated, she was issued an orange jump suit, jailhouse slippers
and cheap hygiene items. She was led to a pod to begin the
dreadful night in the cold of her lonely cell. Woeful anticipation
was interrupted by fitful sleep. Déjà vu.

THE FOLLOWING MORNING when Salty was escorted to
Jas' cell, she looked like a train wreck. Salty entered and sat
down next to her on the cot. He started to say something but
Jas put her hand over his mouth and whispered, "Shhhhh, this
time I'm Shahrazad. I'll tell the story."

"NO! Don't say a word," Salty said with authority. "You
don't have to; I don't want to know. Your case has been dismissed with prejudice. You can never be retried for the same
crime regardless of circumstances–even so-called *newly discovered evidence*. You can only be retried if the case had been dismissed *without* prejudice. There is no need for you to explain
anything to me or to anyone else."

"But...," Jas tried to interrupt.

Salty prevailed and continued, "If the DA decides to re-file
the case, we will obtain a writ to prohibit prosecution and even
take it to the highest court in the land if need be, the United
States Supreme Court. The U.S. Constitution, more particularly, the Fifth Amendment, clearly states that no one can be tried
twice for the same crime. To bring charges again would result in
placing you in *double jeopardy* which, as I say, is a no-no.

"But I… " Jas began but quickly aborted when she saw the stern look on Salty's face. "Okay, you're my attorney and I will take your advice."

"Smart Lady! Who do those clowns think they are? I'm going to obtain your release as soon as possible. We may have to wait for Cooper to make her decision on recharging. If she is as smart as I give her credit for, she will pass on this one. At any rate, we will be able to bail you out pending any appeal in the event the judge allows a refiling."

"Sam, I want you to…"

"NO! Don't ever mention it again. Am I clear on that point? Never again!"

Jas was confused. *Why is he so adamant about not wanting to know the facts? Well, at least I won't have to face the humiliation of explaining what really happened.*

SALTY WAS ALSO conflicted. *I love her so much, I don't want her confession to come between us. I have a pretty good idea of what happened and I don't need the gory details. There's nothing she can reveal that will change my feelings for her–not even complicity.*

As he prepared to leave, Salty took her hand and squeezed it in a gesture of support and confidence. She squeezed back what Salty interpreted as her trust and, also he hoped, her love.

BRIDGES SPENT THE better part of an hour on the phone with Cooper anxiously outlining the newly discovered evidence, which consisted mainly of the inscription on the ring and the incriminating photo album. Cooper listened with intense interest and, knowing it was a long shot, decided to move to refile the case based on the newly discovered evidence.

"Bridges, I'll probably be the laughing stock but, dammit, I'm going to give it a try. I can't stomach the thought of her getting away with cold blooded murder!"

"You know, Cooper, we'll both sleep better knowing we gave it all we had. And, I doubt you'll be the laughing stock. Anyway, not within my earshot."

"You're goofy, but thanks for the support." Then after a long pause, Cooper added, "I was railroaded into agreeing to the dismissal and that still stings."

"I hear that…"

"All right, Bridges, I'll bring the motion with me to Farmington first thing tomorrow. Will you see if you can get us on the docket and inform defense counsel of the date and time of the hearing?"

"My pleasure. I'll make sure we're on the docket."

"Don't get your hopes up. We're travelling in uncharted waters here and the judge may well invoke the barrier erected by the *double jeopardy* clause of the U.S. Constitution."

"I know the ropes. Thanks, Counselor."

WHEN SALTY WAS informed by Detective Bridges that the prosecution was filing a motion to refile the case based on *newly discovered evidence* he didn't know whether to laugh or cry.

The hearing was set for 2:30 p.m. the following afternoon which gave him ample time to prepare his response. With the facts and the law on his side, he was confident the defense would prevail.

He went by the jail to see Jas, after explaining what was about to transpire, he said, "Don't despair. They haven't much of a chance. The Constitution is on our side and that's a pretty powerful ally."

He watched as she sat slumped on her cot occasionally brushing a tear from her cheeks.

"We'll address bond at the hearing and, if all goes well, hopefully have you out of her sometime this afternoon.

At precisely 2:30 p.m., court was called to order and Judge Ralston took the bench.

"I understand there is a motion in the case of *People of the State of New Mexico v. Jasmine Zachary*. Ms. Cooper…"

"Yes, Your Honor. The People have *newly discovered evidence* which further implicates Ms. Zachary as the perpetrator of the crime charged. The prosecution is requesting permission to refile the case in light of this discovery. As Your Honor is aware, Winston Carlton was cleared by law enforcement of having murdered Nick McGregor. His bogus confession, of course, was the basis of the dismissal of the charge previously filed against Ms. Zachary."

Judge Ralston said, "I have a copy of the motion and the defendant's response before me. The response carries a lot of weight regarding *double jeopardy*. However, in the interests of justice, I will grant your motion to refile."

Salty instantly was on his feet. "Judge, may I be heard?"

"Go ahead, Mr. Morton."

"I intend to contest the decision allowing the prosecution leave to refile charges and I will be filing a petition for a Writ of Prohibition with the Supreme Court." Salty rushed on, "In the interim, I'm requesting that the court allow Ms. Zachary to be released from custody on her own recognizance."

The judge peered over his glasses and said, "Mr. Morton, this is a capital case. Do you seriously expect me to grant a PR bond to the defendant? I will, in the alternative, set bond at $200,000."

Stinging from the refusal, Salty said, "Thank you, Your Honor." *Why the hell am I thanking him? Restraint is the better part of valor and I'd be held in contempt if I said what I'm really thinking.*

"Ms. Cooper, do you have anything else?"

"No, Your Honor."

"Mr. Morton?"

"Nothing at this time Your Honor," Salty responded solemnly as he sat mentally composing his writ.

Before they parted, Salty looked at Jas and told her he would see about bail. The appellate process could take a while and he didn't want her sitting in jail another six months.

"Jas, I have a cousin who is bondsman. I'm going to talk to him."

Jas managed a weak smile before she was led back to jail by a matron.

After leaving the courthouse, Salty called "Williams Bail Bonds" and talked to Butch Williams, his cousin and sole owner of the company.

"Hey, Butch, how goes the battle?"

"Salty, you old dog, where ya been?"

"Busy, my friend, very busy. I have a favor to ask you. Have you been following the Zachary murder case?"

"Hasn't everyone?"

"Yeah. Good point. Well, as you know Jas is my client."

"Doesn't everyone?"

Salty ignored the sarcastic remark and continued, "The prosecution just filed a motion which was granted to refile the case on the basis of *newly discovered evidence*. When the case was dismissed the first time, jeopardy attached and no matter what the circumstances, Jas cannot constitutionally be retried for the same crime. However, she has been rearrested pending the outcome of the writ I am seeking to obtain from the Supreme Court regarding *double jeopardy*."

"Okay, I'm tracking with ya," Butch said.

"Good! The judge has set bond at $200,000. If you would post bond to get her released, I will guarantee that you will not lose your money. I would post it myself but I don't have immediate access to that much cash or sureties on such short notice and I don't want to see Jas remain in jail over the weekend. I know you have assets on hand because that's your business. What say you?"

"Salty, old man, since you're a blood relative, and even if you weren't, I trust you when you say you do not intend to lose. So, out of respect, deference, courtesy and kinship, I will do it. I'm also counting on you giving your word that the defendant will not flee the state pending the outcome of the hearing."

Salty breathed a sigh of relief. "Butch, you have my word and I will make sure that does not happen. If for some unforeseen reason it does, I will personally reimburse you the amount of the bond. Also, I will have my runner deliver a check to you for $20,000.00 representing the 10% bond premium the minute I hang up. I owe you one, Cuz. Thanks."

"You owe me nothing. Well, maybe a beer next time I see ya.

"More like a case of Michelob."

Butch laughed, "Take care. I'll get over to the courthouse within the hour and do everything I can to expedite the process."

And so he did. Jas was released from jail on bond later that day and Salty was there to pick her up and be at her side as he had been from the beginning–and not just physically but in mind and heart as well.

AS THEY WERE preparing to leave the jail, Jas, having retrieved her personal belongings, once again placed the small gold cross pendant around her neck.

While toying with it she said, "Sam, I have never had the opportunity to pay my last respects to Nick. Would it be too much to ask you to take me by the cemetery so I may say a proper goodbye?"

"Of course I'll take you," Salty replied. "Are you sure that's something you want to do in light of what you've already been through?"

"Yes, I'm sure," Jas replied with resolve. "I think personally saying goodbye would provide me some closure to this nightmare. With all that has happened, this would ease my conscience." *Paying my respects, plus going to confession and atoning for my many sins is the least I can do! Oh, God, I'm so very sorry I killed him. If only I could undo what I have done and change the course of history.*

"Hey, where'd you go?" Salty asked. "I lost you there for a minute."

Jas looked at Salty, her eyes dampened, "I was just thinking about the past two years and how fast one's life can change. I know I haven't told you how very much I appreciate you defending me and having faith and trust in me. Appreciate is not even close to what I feel for you but for lack of a better word..."

Tears now flowed freely down her cheeks and Salty took her in his arms and after his tender consolation and tears of his own, Jas continued, "Sam, I would not have made it without you. You kept me going these last five months. Cooped up in solitude, I looked so forward to your visits. They were the only bright spot in my day. When I was ready to hang it up and just give up, you would appear with your upbeat attitude and buoy me up. It was you who gave me the inspiration, courage and hope to continue.

"Throughout my life I've always thought it was important to tell the people in your life how you felt about them: your parents, your husband, your kids, your friends and, of course, your lovers. I've learned that just thinking someone knows or should know, without you actually verbally expressing your feelings, can lead to severe misunderstandings and often result in unintended consequences. I can't even put into words how I feel about you and all you mean to me."

"Hey," Salty replied while still holding Jas in his arms, "you're my client. That's the least I could do. Besides, you deserved it." Salty was hesitant to bear his own soul at this time knowing that Jas was referring to Nick, her past relationship with Nick and the guilt she felt for having killed him all because of misunderstandings, unwarranted assumptions and impulsiveness.

When they arrived at the cemetery, they headed in the direction of the mausoleum and Salty waited for her in the car. Jas was so emotional her legs shook as she made her way to the site. When she saw Nick's name on the brass plate attached to the cement square that sealed his ashes inside the small compartment she began to weep. Then grief-stricken, she fell to her knees. Her body racked with sobs. "Oh, Nick, I'm so sorry. Oh, my darling, I'm so, so sorry. I miss you so much and always will." After remaining in this position for a long period, she ultimately regained her composure. What was done, was done! She'd give anything to take it all back but life goes on. She stood up, wiped her eyes, straightened her clothing and turned to leave. As she approached the wrought iron gate adorned with two winged angles standing guard over the cemetery, she turned and, looking back at the place where Nick's remains rested, threw him her signature departing kiss for the last time. "Goodbye, my darling; rest in peace. I will love you forever."

ON THE RIDE home, Salty said, "I haven't eaten all day and I'm beginning to fade. How 'bout we have lunch?"

Jas flashed him a quick shy smile, "Suddenly, I, too, am ravenous. Let's do. I'm not looking forward to facing the mess the police created when they rummaged through my home."

They stopped at a restaurant that was still serving breakfast. Bacon, eggs, pancakes and hot coffee sounded like heaven and they both ate heartedly.

Salty occasionally would catch Jas staring at him while they ate.

I can't stand the suspense so I'm just going to ask him. "Why don't you want to know what really had happened?" She sat nervously toying with the small gold cross pendant waiting for Salty's response.

Salty simply said, "I want to get to know you outside the realm of attorney/client. I want to take you places and experience a life with you in which I've never let myself indulge. In case you didn't know, I've fallen in love with you and my fondest hope is that you could love me, too." He looked into those big blue eyes searching for a glimmer of encouragement.

Suddenly, she surprised him by jumping up and throwing her arms around his neck and kissing him full on the lips. "Oh, Sam! Let's give ourselves a chance to be happy together. I would very much like that. Please be patient and give me time to heal. I'm trying to fight my attraction to you but its not working. You're too irresistible."

SALTY'S HEART SOARED with the expectation that Jas could set aside the past and open herself up and thereby give their relationship a chance to grow into love.

After lunch, Salty dropped Jas off at her condo and returned to his office to prepare his writ of prohibition and memorandum of authority, which turned out to be a piece of cake considering he had the facts, the undisputed law and the United States Constitution on his side.

Salty was so encouraged and excited about pursuing a relationship with Jas that he could hardly wait to invite her out. He had dated in the past but only casually and no one had ever affected him the way Jas did.

The next day he called.

"Hello," she answered.

"Hey, haven't seen you in," Salty said and, looking at his watch, added "at least fourteen hours. I'm going into withdrawal. How would you like to join me for dinner this evening?"

Jas laughed, "Can't think of anything I'd rather do."

Jas, having been incarcerated for so long, was more than eager to have some fun. She had lost so much weight while incarcerated that her clothes no longer fit nor, for that matter, suited the occasion. Desiring to look her best, she spent the afternoon shopping for a new wardrobe.

Salty was punctual and Jas was ready when he arrived. When she opened the door, sporting a new hair style, dressed in a sleek black skirt and a white silk blouse, he exclaimed, "You're stunning."

Jas pirouetted. Salty, stricken by her natural beauty, said, "I like the transition. You could not look lovelier!"

Jas blushed and said, "That's a nice thing to say. And, you Sir, look most handsome."

Salty was not ordinarily bashful but to hear this kind of compliment, especially from this beautiful creature, was unnerving to say the least. He felt an excitement he thought was reserved only for the young.

There was an awkward moment when neither uttered a word. But then again they didn't need to. Their eyes said it all!

"Well, Prince Charming," Jas finally said, "where are you carrying me off to?"

"Not where I'd like to. But then again maybe that's something to look forward to."

Jas was not quite sure if she heard Sam right and didn't have a clever quip. So, she just smiled and filed his comment away for the moment–at least for the *proper* moment.

"Oh, sorry," Salty said. "I assume you are asking where I'm taking you for dinner."

"It's your call. Never do your decisions disappoint."

"I hear they have great prime rib at The River Side. Does that sound good to you?"

Jas froze. *That's where Nick and I had our first date and where Nick's daughters had the surprise birthday party. Dining there would only revive memories which I don't care to revisit. I need a fresh start. The past with Nick is the past; my future with Sam starts now.*

"Know what, Sam, after all the bland meals I had in jail, I've been craving Mexican food. I think I'd really like to go to *Francisco's*."

"Ah ha, you do have good taste. That really hits the spot with me. *Francisco's* is my all-time favorite restaurant. So, *Francisco's* it is!"

Salty extended his arm and escorted Jas to his vehicle. Jas appeared to be somewhat subdued on the ride to the restaurant. However, once they were seated and the margaritas sampled she became more relaxed and conversant.

The couple did not escape the attention of the other diners, many of whom they both knew. A few stopped and engaged in casual chatter. However, for the most part Salty and Jas were given the cold shoulder and, from the sly and covert looks shot their way, they suspected they were the subject of idle gossip.

"Is this getting too uncomfortable for you?" Salty asked.

Jas looked down. After a moment she snapped her head back up, "No! I'm not going to capitulate and let the gossip mongers win."

Salty reached across the table and grasped her hand. She continued, "I expected as much and, with you here with me, I feel brave enough to face it." Suddenly, a look of concern crossed Jas' face, "How about you?"

"You kidding me," Salty chuckled. "Like the man said, one just can't get enough publicity and, from the looks of things, I'm getting plenty."

SALTY, HAVING NEVER married and having a thriving law practice, amassed a virtual fortune. That was common knowledge. He had enough for the two to live on comfortably, even extravagantly, for the rest of their lives. He wasn't worried about the adverse consequences that might be generated because of his involvement with a former client especially one charged with first degree murder. After all, the charge was ultimately dismissed. Regardless, he didn't care at this stage in his career what people thought.

Salty reveled in how radiant Jas looked in the candle light. It was as though it was magnifying the newfound happiness within. The evening was filled with excited anticipation. Their first date heralded in a new season of unprecedented romance, a romance Salty hoped would endure the test of time.

WITHIN A WEEK after her release from jail, Jas drove to Aztec to confess her sins as required by her faith. She deliberately picked an obscure church some distance away where she wouldn't be recognized. Anonymity, in her situation, was, to her, crucial. Although the Catholic Church had started using face-to-face confessionals several years before, one could still remain incognito by kneeling behind the screen that separated the priest from the penitent rather than the face-to-face concept. There was little likelihood that she would be recognized in Aztec. She was basically driven by her conscious to make this confession. She thought if she died with so many mortal sins on her soul she would surely spend eternity in hell.

Before embarking on her quest, Jas researched the Catholic dictates concerning the Seal of Confession and learned that priests could not disclose anything they heard from penitents during the course of the Sacrament of Penance. To do so, would result in excommunication of the priest. Jas breathed a sigh of relief learning that she could confess and not be subject to legal recrimination. Even though jeopardy had attached, she still was not secure in the belief that she was totally free — especially since she had already been arrested twice for the same crime and was possibly facing a second prosecution.

Jas found the church easily enough as she had been there with Yvonne once or twice in the past. San Jose, a Spanish-style church, had been dedicated over a century before. It had an exterior of beige stucco and seven steps leading to the massive double front doors fashioned out of hewn oak logs with brass hardware. There was a steeple on the roof which housed an old bell that had come from a church that had been burned in Aqua Prieta, Sonora, Mexico. The bell was transported by the faithful to New Mexico to remind them of their Mexican roots and especially their ancestors who had died in the fire.

The fire was suspicious and thought to have been set purposefully by rebels protesting the Holy See's stand on various issues. The doors to the old church had been bolted from the outside preventing the parishioners from escaping. Approximately one hundred and fifty men, women and children suffered a horrific death standing up for their faith. The source of the fire was never determined. The remainder of the small community, being in fear for their own lives, packed up their belongings, including the charred bell from the burned-out church and made their way to New Mexico. Eventually they built another San Jose, a church named after that church in Aqua Prieta.

The masonry and carpentry were intricate and masterful considering the meager tools with which the small band had to work. The pews were hand-carved and the altar was honed from the natural stone found in the surrounding foothills. The statues of Mary, Joseph and Baby Jesus were created by the women in much the same fashion as they created pottery. One of the survivors was an artist who painted the statues so expertly that they appeared life-like. They were captivating and revered. The crucifix was carved from roughhewn oak and the crucified Jesus was created and painted in the same fashion as the other icons. Miraculously, the paint had not faded or chipped over time. Those who view the finished product know beyond all doubt that deity had a hand in the creation which stood sentinel at the entrance of the church protecting those within. When one walked past the statue of St. Joseph, his eyes seemed to follow and only distance would interrupt his gazes.

The interior of the church was cool and dim. The only light came from the stained glass windows, the rack of votive candles that were lit by loved ones to gain indulgences for the faithfully departed, and the eternal light that burned to the right of the altar at the foot of the statue of the Blessed Virgin Mother. The crucifix was suspended above the altar depicting a suffering Christ dying on the cross a symbol of the redemption of sin.

UPON ENTERING THE church, Jas genuflected and made the sign of the cross. She observed a line of penitents waiting their turn in the confessional. She joined the line. She winced at the thought of the evil she had perpetrated. She was truly sorry for having offended her Lord and prayed for the strength to get through her confession without faltering. Soon it was her turn. Her stomach churned and she wondered if she was going to be sick. Steeling herself against the urge to flee, she entered the confessional.

The priest was cordial and invited her to begin her confession. Fearing she would lose her resolve, she blurted out everything she mentally rehearsed hardly stopping to take a breath and then dissolved into tears.

The stunned young priest was speechless. This was the first time anyone had confessed to him of having committed a homicide. He didn't know how to proceed so he asked her for details. She said she would rather not expound on the circumstances. She was here to get absolved of her sins for which she was truly sorry and repentant. The priest was silent for a long period as he sat reflecting and praying for guidance. He ultimately concluded that, according to scripture, on the road to Damascus, Jesus interacted with Saul, forgave him for killing Christians, changed Saul's name to Paul and commissioned him to spread the good news. How could he, a humble priest and servant of God, do less than Jesus?

Waiting, Jas fidgeted. *Is he trying to decide whether or not to forgive me? I shouldn't have come… There I go again trying to read anothers' thoughts and feelings. That's how I got into this mess in the first place.*

The priest finally said he would absolve her of her sin but her penance would be great. He didn't know if this was protocol or not but sensed it was divine intervention so he told Jas she would have to make recompense to the victim's family in some fashion and say a rosary every day for a year for the repose of the soul of her victim.

Thank you Lord. I expected much more in the way of penance. I would have agreed to anything.

After making a perfect Act of Contrition, Jas left the confessional. She slid into a pew in the rear of the church. Making the familiar sign of the cross, she silently prayed, *"Thank you God for giving me the strength to follow through with my confession. I feel like the weight of the world has been lifted from my shoulders. I know I will have to atone for my transgression in Purgatory but you know my heart and that I am truly sorry for having sinned against you. I include Nick in my Act of Contrition. Please forgive him. He didn't have a chance to repent. I robbed him of that. Not only did I kill him but I may have stole paradise from him as well. Loving, merciful and gracious Father, I beseech you to make allowances for Nick. I promise that I will live the rest of my life making up for the severe damage I've caused. Please, dear God, send me a sign that Nick is forgiven. I will not rest until I know. I ask this in Jesus' name. Amen.*

Jas slowly stood and made her way to the exit. She crossed herself with holy water and looking back towards the confessional, issued a sigh of relief. She then turned and moved out into the sunlight. As she stood on the steps adjusting to the brightness of the day, a group of school children filed past under the watchful eye of an elderly nun. Jas watched as they passed.

Still watching, Jas saw one of the young boys turn and, as though the miracle she asked for was manifesting itself before her very eyes, the child threw her a kiss mirroring the traditional departure kiss she ceremoniously threw to Nick throughout their relationship. She also noticed the boy's smile. It was a smile etched in her memory–Nick's smile.

A stunned Jas turned back toward the church, folded her hands together in prayer and said aloud, "Thank you, God. Thank you. Thank you. Thank you." Jas had turned toward the church only momentarily. When she looked back to where she had observed the young boy, she could scarcely believe her eyes, not by what she saw, but by what she didn't see. There was no sign of the boy or anyone else. All had disappeared as quickly as they had appeared.

ON THE DRIVE home, still in disbelief pondering the mystery of what had just occurred, Jas wondered what she could do for recompense to Nicole and Nick's other daughters. It was important to her to satisfy her penance as soon as possible; especially in light of having experienced what she believed was a miracle. Suddenly she had an epiphany. *I'll sell the ring and split the proceeds between the four girls. That's all I have of any value. My savings had been depleted during the five months I spent in jail. I still didn't know if and what Sam is going to charge for my defense. Nor, do I know what a diamond that size is worth. Regardless, it should be part of his daughters' inheritance. Parting with it will be extremely painful. It's the only proof I have of Nick's love for me. Then again, perhaps pain is part of my penance. I don't need anything tangible by which to remember Nick. His memory will forever be etched in my heart, mind and soul. Well, that decision was easy. I'll sell the ring as soon as possible and anonymously distribute the proceeds to Nick's daughters.*

SALTY READ AND reread his petition for a writ of prohibition and at the end of the day he decided the document was all-inclusive and met all the legal requirements. The basic fundamental right of all American citizens, he would remind the court, was the right not to be tried twice for the same crime thus to not be placed in *double jeopardy*. Salty was more than pleased with his creation. He express mailed the original of the document accompanied by ten copies to the New Mexico Supreme Court. He filed a copy with the San Juan County District Court and mailed another copy to Cooper.

Cooper's response and brief in opposition to Salty's petition was filed well in advance of the deadline. That in itself was miraculous as filing anything early was unheard of. Attorneys were notorious for pressing up against deadlines and pressuring themselves and their staffs into ulcers and heart attacks. Her response rested on equitable grounds since there was not much else. It read:

> The ends of justice, in light of the newly discovered incriminatory evidence, cries out for prosecution. The greatest good for the greatest number should trump a guilty individual's claim of double jeopardy. No one is above the law and no one should profit from his or her own misdeeds.

Salty was confident his argument that Cooper's response was moot in light of the constitutional right not to be tried twice for the same crime would stand up even at the State Supreme Court level. Thus began the long agonizing wait.

After the first week, Salty checked the mail no less than daily hoping for an opinion which he knew would not be rendered for some weeks. The court's docket was always backlogged but Salty was anxious. Jas' freedom was hanging in the balance. At the end of the fifth week the opinion was finally posted. Salty carelessly tore open the envelope and hastily thumbed to the last page. There he read the high court's opinion:

> **THE COURT FINDS,** in accordance with the Constitution of New Mexico and the Constitu-

tion of the United States as follows: The case of *People of the State of New Mexico, Plaintiff v. Jasmine Zachary, Defendant,* cannot be reinstated nor the aforesaid Defendant retried. This Court upholds the Defendant's position as outlined in her petition for Writ of Prohibition. Our ruling is that jeopardy attached upon dismissal with prejudice at the first trial and to reinstate the case or retry the Defendant would result in double jeopardy which is clearly in violation of the Constitution of the State of New Mexico as well as the Constitution of the United States.

IT IS THE COURT'S ORDER, therefore, that the Defendant, Jasmine Zachary, be and is hereby exonerated and declared immune from criminal prosecution on the pending charges. The motion, therefore, is denied and the case against the Defendant is hereby dismissed with prejudice for all time never again to be resurrected.

DONE BY THE COURT:

/s/ Corbin J. Dominguez_____

Chief Justice of the New Mexico Supreme Court

EPILOGUE

Okay, people, that's a wrap." Bishop shouted to the *Sincerely Yours* crew. Her team jumped into action, yanking on cords and disassembling lights and camera stands. Bishop rose, and extending her hand, said, "Thank you, Salty, for the interview. What a fascinating story. It will be a few weeks before we actually air the segment. I'll let you know the exact date and time so you can watch."

Bishop furrowed her brow as she stuffed a sheaf of papers into her valise and fastened the clasp. She picked up her oversized bag, slung it over her shoulder and looked around ensuring she had all of her belongings. As she turned to leave, she hesitated for a moment and turned back. Looking at Salty, she said, "Okay, don't leave me hanging on this one. You've got to tell me, what happened to your client?"

At that exact moment, the door to the reception area swung open and an auburn haired beauty swept into the room. Bishop watched as Salty rounded his desk going out to greet the visitor and lightly kissing the woman's cheek before escorting her to his office.

"Linda," Salty said, "I'd like to introduce you to my wife, Jasmine Zachary Morton." Then, he added, with pride in his voice, "You may have read her novel, *Beguiled.*"

Bishop blinked and then her eyes grow wide as she stood in silence connecting the dots. *Salty's wife is the infamous Jasmine Zachary. Well, I'll be damned.*

Finding her voice, Bishop finally said as she extended her right hand, "Mrs. Morton, I'm pleased to meet you. I have read *Beguiled* and... I liked it, I liked it very much, but..."

Before Bishop could complete her sentence, Salty interrupted, "Jas, this is Linda Bishop, a reporter from *Sincerely Yours.*" Then he gestured toward the camera crew as they began shouldering their black canvas bags preparing to leave, "As you can see, we just finished an interview featuring my most interesting career case." He hesitated momentarily, then asked, "Can you guess which one I chose, dear?"

Jas smiled and took Bishop's hand, "A pleasure to meet you, Ms. Bishop. And, thank you, I'm pleased to hear you liked my novel." Jas then looked up at Salty, and toying with the small gold cross pendant suspended around her neck, replied, "Please tell me, Sam, which case did you chose?"

"The one with the happy ending," Salty replied, gazing into her sparkling big blue eyes, "the one with the happy ending."

... and so it ends...

ABOUT THE AUTHOR

Judith Blevins' entire professional life was spent experiencing the mystery, intrigue and drama that unfold daily within the criminal justice system. Her previous experience as a court clerk, and then serving five consecutive district attorneys, has provided the inspiration for her stories. Blevins, now retired, lives in Grand Junction, Colorado, and continues to write mystery/romance novels. She and fellow fiction writer, Carroll Multz, have coauthored a series of children/young adult novels featuring the R*U*1*2s, a band of preteens who collaborate to solve mysteries.

Made in the USA
Charleston, SC
09 April 2016